An Unlikely Partnership

A. K. Gentry

Brushy Mountain Publications

For permission requests, contact Brushy Mountain Publications, Statesville, NC,   email: brushymtnpub@gmail.com

ISBN 979-8-9888618-0-5 (Paperback)

ISBN 979-8-9888618-1-2 (Digital)

Library of Congress Control Number: 2023944580

Book Cover by Marissa Mueller at MAM Crafted
Instagram @mamcrafted1

Printed in the United States of America

Acknowledgements

I would like to thank Wanda Collins, Jennie Gentry, Jimmy Gentry, and Gay Shaver for their time and suggestions in the process of proofreading and editing.

I would also like to thank Missy Mueller for her talent and her patience with me as she developed the book cover.

Contents

Chapter 1

M egan Albright surveyed her reflection in the mirror. Her chestnut hair, streaked with natural auburn highlights, was swept upward in a tidy bun. Pulling her hair back from her face and using taupe eye shadow highlighted her green eyes. Her favorite lipstick, which reminded her of a robin's red breast, was the finishing touch to her makeup.

The white sandals Megan wore were slightly over two inches in the heel, bringing her to a slender five feet seven inches. Standing back from the mirror she let her friends, Allie Stone and Candy Cotton, fasten the veil to the top of her head. Today she would become Mrs. Chip Garner.

Megan met Chip when he came to Whitlow from Philadelphia to be the best man in Allie and Jacob Stone's wedding. Jacob was originally from Philadelphia but had moved to Whitlow because of an unusual inheritance. The situation threw Allie and Jacob into close contact with each other, and they had fallen in love. Megan was glad because otherwise, she would have never met Chip.

"You look beautiful!" Allie said with sincerity.

"Yes," agreed Candy. "Your gown is perfect for you. I hope if I ever get married, I will be half as beautiful as you are."

Megan looked at Candy and said, "That is so sweet, thank you. But don't say if, say when. Your time will come."

"I think you're ready," Allie said. "I hear the prelude starting. It won't be long."

Megan smiled, "I guess we just wait until we are summoned by the wedding director."

Not wanting to wrinkle the gown, Megan stood in the bride's room of the church and looked out over the grounds behind the fellowship hall. Her thoughts drifted back to meeting Chip.

Chip had introduced himself to her at Allie's wedding as Jacob's best friend. The moment Megan saw him, she knew she wanted to get to know him. He was slightly over six feet tall with dark brown hair and brown eyes that had a slight gold tone in the sunlight. He was lean and muscled from his active job as a building contractor, but his smile was what drew her to him. That wide smile with straight white teeth put a twinkle in his eye that was irresistible.

The wedding planner knocked on the door and said, "We're ready for you ladies."

Megan grinned at her friends and said, "Let's go to a wedding."

Chapter 2

C hip Garner fastened the cuff links onto his shirt
then put his coat on. He turned to his friend, Jacob,
and his brother, Paul, and asked, "How do I look?"

Jacob snickered.

"What?" Chip asked.

Paul rolled his eyes and said, "Little brother, you never
did know how to properly knot a tie."

Paul, who was six feet and three inches in height,
leaned down to his brother, unknotted the tie, and retied
it in a perfect knot to go with his tuxedo.

"Thanks, Bro," Chip said to Paul. He grinned, "You always did look after me. Why should I learn to knot a tie
when you were always there to do it?"

"Because," Paul replied, "I'm not going to be there anymore. Your wife will be, and unless she knows how to do
that, you're up the creek, buddy."

He paused then asked, "Are you sure you want to do
this? We can always sneak out the back."

"I'm not listening to this," Jacob said, raising his hands
in a stopping motion. "Allie would kill me if she even

suspected I knew you were going to do that."

Chip laughed, "No worries, Jacob.

There's no way I would miss the chance to marry Megan Albright. I'm head over heels in love and proud of it."

The three men paused when they heard the prelude starting in the church sanctuary. Chip grinned as he listened. He thought back to when he met Megan. It was at another wedding. He was Jacob's best man, and she was Allie's maid of honor.

There had been no rehearsal for the wedding, so the first time he saw Megan was when she walked down the aisle ahead of Allie. He was so mesmerized he forgot to breathe for at least ten seconds. He knew at that moment he was going to marry her. For him it had been love at first sight.

Allie and Jacob's wedding had been so small they had not even walked back down the aisle. They just stood in place while everyone came forward to wish them well. Chip stood back to watch the group and asked the pastor for the name of the maid of honor. Then Chip walked around the happy couple and introduced himself to Megan. He was so taken with her that he asked Rich Hayes, the family friend who was letting him stay at his home, if he could stay an extra night.

Instead of going home that Sunday, he went with Rich to church, asked Megan to lunch, and the two spent the rest of the day getting to know each other. He made frequent trips back to Whitlow and finally applied for a business license in North Carolina. When he had the license in his hands, he showed it to Megan and asked her to marry him.

Her response was, "Yes! I thought you'd never ask!"

Pastor Ken broke Chip's reverie when he said, "It's time. We need to go to the front of the church."

Out of a side door, Pastor Ken, Chip, Jacob, and Paul walked in front of the right side of pews to the aisle and waited. First down the aisle was Candy and then Allie. The wedding guests stood as Megan was escorted down the aisle by her father.

The marriage ceremony was traditional and brief. Soon Chip and Megan were married. When Chip kissed Megan in front of the church, Jacob looked at Allie and smiled, remembering their own wedding. At the same time, Paul looked over at Candy. She was watching the bride and groom with a slightly wistful expression.

Candy absently smiled as she watched Chip kiss his bride. It made her slightly sad that both her friends were married, and she wasn't. When Candy looked away, Paul was able to catch her eye and raise an eyebrow as if reading her thoughts. Candy rolled her eyes and turned her head. She thought Chip was great, but his brother was annoying. How could two brothers be so different. Chip was the perfect height, smiled constantly, was outgoing, and everyone who met him liked him.

On the other hand, Candy thought Paul was overly

tall and broad. His black hair was slightly too long, and his blue eyes always seemed to be hooded, never letting anyone see what he was feeling. She would be glad when he left town. He made her feel like someone was scraping their nails down a blackboard whenever she had to interact with him.

Candy gave an involuntary shiver and turned her thoughts back to the wedding. Annoyed, Candy realized the wedding party was leaving the front of the church, and she was going to have to take Paul's arm.

Candy watched Allie take Jacob's arm as they walked back down the aisle. She moved forward, gave Paul a fake smile, took his arm loosely, and walked to the back of the church to join the wedding party.

Paul almost laughed out loud when he saw the smirk Candy gave him. He knew she had taken an instant dislike to him, but that made her intriguing. Usually, he had to be creative to keep away from women. He had never had one try to keep away from him.

When the reception was over, the new couple laughingly ran through a shower of birdseed, got into their car and drove away. Candy was at the back of the crowd watching. It had been deliberate on her part because there was no way she wanted to catch that bouquet when Megan threw it.

She sighed deeply. The event was over, and she could stop being nice and outgoing. That was always stressful. No one knew that she was an introvert because she was so friendly at the café, but that was a job, not a personality statement.

Paul leaned against the doorframe of the church. He appeared to be watching the birdseed shower, but he was, in fact, watching Candy. She was an enigma to him and full of secrets. It was evident that being outgoing was stressful for her. He bet no one paid enough attention to her to realize she had the traits of an introvert.

Candy was only a few feet in front of him.

He asked, "Are you glad it's over?"

Candy jumped slightly, startled that someone was behind her. She turned. Oh wonderful, she thought sarcastically, the annoying brother.

She answered, "It was nice, but yes, I'm glad it's over. I'm tired."

"I can tell," Paul said.

Again, Candy was annoyed that Paul of all people had been able to see through her smile and conversation to the fatigue beneath it.

She said, "Well, I'm going home to put on a movie, eat popcorn, and not speak until tomorrow."

"What's tomorrow?" he asked.

"Work," Candy answered.

"Ah, yes. The old grind. What do you do, if I may ask?"

"I own a café in town. Breakfast begins at six in the morning. I usually open to make sure everything goes smoothly for the day. So, I need to go. Bye. Have a safe trip to wherever you live."

Candy turned to walk back to the bride's room and retrieve her belongings.

Paul chuckled. She was feisty. Well, it might be a good idea to have breakfast at the café before he left town in the morning.

Chapter 3

P aul rose early the next morning and did his usual workout in the exercise room of the motel where he was staying. He had been offered a room at several homes for the weekend, but he liked his own space.

Paul was comfortable in his own skin. The reason he recognized Candy's introverted qualities was because he had them himself. Being pleasant, talkative and altogether social was tiring. Besides, he couldn't just ask for time out to exercise if he was staying at someone's home. A daily workout was essential to Paul's physical and mental health.

Having been an athlete in high school, Paul had gone to college on a basketball scholarship. He started teaching, hoping to coach basketball, but he soon found that the daily grind of a set job was not in his makeup. The students were great. Paul liked them and they liked him, but having to be at the same place at the same time every day was stressful and boring.

It was during that time he began to use exercise to relieve stress. Now, he enjoyed his job, but he still liked the stress relieving endorphins he achieved from working out.

After he left teaching, Paul took a truck driving course and began working for a company in Philadelphia. Driving was fine, but he found he liked the logistics side of the company better. He stopped driving, learned the management side of the business, then started his own company.

Paul contracted with vendors and trucking companies. He supplied the vendors with freight carriers which then supplied the trucking companies with freight. It was a challenging puzzle and the most fun he ever had on a job. The beauty of the job was that he could work from anywhere as long as he had his computer and a cell phone.

Paul took his cellphone and looked up the café in Whitlow. Candy's Café. He smiled. To him she looked like someone who should be named Candy. Her hair was so blond it was almost white and full of tight natural curls, but those eyes. They were a vivid blue that a man could get lost in. He also liked the fact that she wasn't too short since he was so tall.

Paul grinned. If he walked into that café and she was wearing a pink uniform, he would laugh out loud. He noticed on her website that she had Wi-Fi for customers. Perfect. He could get some work done while he checked out Candy and her café.

Paul arranged to keep his room at the hotel for another night then drove into Whitlow. It was only a few minutes after seven, so he had his pick of the parking places on Main Street. He chose one that was a few slots away from the front door then walked inside.

A waitress behind the counter said, "Welcome to Candy's. Sit wherever you want."

Paul looked around the long room. He chose a booth across from the counter. The waitresses behind the counter had access to the food, drinks, flatware, and most importantly, coffee. He smiled as the young woman, who said her name was Tina, handed him a menu. He asked for coffee while he decided what to order.

Tina brought his coffee. Paul gave her his order and asked for the Wi-Fi password. He opened his computer, logged onto the service, and checked his emails. There were several requests for trucking services from his most frequent vendors. Paul used a split screen to check which trucks were available and emailed the managers of those companies. By the time his food arrived, Paul had arranged freight transportation for two of the vendors. He smiled. Two sets of happy customers.

Paul looked up to see Candy setting his plate on the table.

"Mr. Garner," she said, "To what do I owe the pleasure of your patronage this morning?"

"Just checking out the local cuisine," he said with a smile. "And you have Wi-Fi. I can get a little work done while I eat and drink a couple cups of coffee."

"Marvelous. Well, enjoy your meal."

Candy turned and walked back behind the counter. She never gave him a second glance.

Paul frowned slightly. Getting to know Candy Cotton was going to take persistence and luck. While eating, Paul kept his eyes on both his computer and Candy. She was an efficient manager, and she appeared to be genuinely caring about both her employees and the customers. He guessed it was because she knew everyone, Whitlow being a small town.

Tina took his plate and kept his coffee cup full. After another half hour of work, Paul noticed the café was almost full of diners. Looking around, he saw only two vacant booths. He closed his laptop and opened his wallet to take out money for a generous tip.

Paul had been so engrossed in his work that he hadn't noticed the change in the mood of the employees. They looked tense. In an office at the very end of the room, he could see Candy talking with a man and a woman. No one was arguing. If anything, the couple looked like they were apologizing to Candy.

Taking his time, Paul was able to get up just as the couple was leaving. Candy left her office, and two of the servers rushed over. One hugged her, and the other just patted her on the back. What was happening?

Paul took his check and money to Tina at the cash register. In a quiet voice, Paul asked, "What just happened?

The mood in here changed, and Candy looks upset."

Tina looked around then said in a low tone, "Those were the landlords. They're selling the building, and they wanted to let Candy know. There isn't a buyer. They just want to sell out and move to Florida. No one knows if the new owner will let Candy keep her café or if they'll use the building for another purpose. It's stressful."

"No doubt," Paul said. He smiled, "I'm in town for another day, so I'll probably see you for dinner."

Tina smiled back, "Not me. I get off at two. Candy's the only one who ever works from opening to closing."

"Well, have a good day, then," Paul said, and he left.

Paul sat in his car looking at the building that housed the café. There was a second story, but it seemed unoccupied. He started the car then drove around the block to see the back side of the building. There was only one door. He wondered how the upstairs was accessed.

Using his cell phone, Paul looked up the tax records and history on the building. Then he pulled the property up on a realty website. It was already listed. Paul blinked twice. He could not believe the price. He was so used to the high cost of living in Philadelphia that anything priced less came as a shock.

Paul pondered the purchase of the building. Was he out of his mind? How could he have gotten so obsessed over a woman who could not stand him, that he was willing to buy a piece of property just to make her life a little easier. Oh well, what could it hurt to look at the building.

The realtor's website said they open at nine. Paul looked at his watch. It was almost nine. The problem was going to be looking at the building when the café was not open. He didn't want Candy to know he was interested in the property.

After giving the matter some thought, he came up with the most logical solution. He would have Chip look at the building and evaluate it at the same time. Chip could make a video call with him and show Paul what the upstairs was like. Then he could have Chip do the renovations, and Jacob could make changes in the plumbing and electrical wiring. The problem was that Chip would not be back from his honeymoon for another three days. He had to have another plan.

Paul grinned, started his car and drove away. A few minutes later he was pulling into the parking lot of Rich Hayes' law office. He walked in and asked the receptionist if he could make an appointment with Rich that day or the next as he was from out of town and needed to get back to where he lived.

Rich heard them talking and came out into the lobby.

Paul saw him and said, "Mr. Hayes, I am Mr. Smith, and I wondered if I could have a moment of your time."

Rich looked quizzically at Paul for a moment then said, "Of course. Come into my office." Rich led him inside and closed the door.

Then he asked, "Mr. Garner, would you like to explain the secrecy of your visit?"

Paul smiled, "Thanks for playing along. I don't want anyone to know I'm here and why."

Rich said, "Alright, what can I do for you?"

"The building that houses Candy's Café has just been put up for sale."

Rich looked surprised. "I had no idea. When did that happen?"

"This morning," Paul said. "I was eating breakfast there when the whole mood in the café changed. The owners came in to break the news to Candy. Whether or not she can keep the café there will be up to the new owner."

"I suppose so," Rich said. "What does this have to do with you?"

"I want to buy the building."

"You want to buy the building?" Rich asked in a shocked voice. "But why? You live in Philadelphia."

Paul smiled. "I'm going to renovate the upstairs into an apartment. Chip is my family, and I am a believer of family staying together. The second reason is that I don't want Candy to lose her café. The reason for the secrecy is that I don't want anyone to know I own the building."

Rich looked at Paul closely. "Alright, I understand the apartment and the family part, but why are you so interested in Candy keeping the café?"

Paul looked back at Rich and said, "Honestly, I'm not completely sure. The food is great, and it's a fixture in Whitlow, but that's not the main reason. The woman hates me. She absolutely cannot stand the air I breathe, and I don't know why."

Paul continued, "I'm not a stalker, or anything like that, but if I live above the café, and she thinks I'm just renting the apartment, maybe I can figure out what the problem is. I hope we can be friends. I mean, she's friends with my sister-in-law. There's no way we will be able to completely avoid each other the rest of our lives, so why not try to make peace."

Rich tried not to smile as he listened to Paul. The man was fascinated with Candy. Well, it would be fun just watching the fireworks.

Rich said, "Alright. Do you want me to handle the purchase?"

"Yes, if you would. Can we do it in such a way that the deed is in my name but the realtor, Candy and owners won't know who is buying it?"

Rich said, "Yes. There are ways that can be done. I will draw up the deed here and register it at the courthouse. You know that is a public record. Anyone who wants to know who owns it can find out through the tax office website."

"Register it in my property company's name. Not even Chip knows that."

"Alright. When do you want to do this?" Rich asked.

"Would you look at the property, take a video, then send it to me? I would like to see it before I make the offer. If it's decent, I'll give them the asking price. If it's a dump, I will give them a low price and negotiate."

Rich said, "Alright. I'll try to do that this afternoon. Give me your phone number."

Paul gave him a business card.

Rich said, "I'll send you the video. How long are you in town?"

Paul answered, "Right now, until tomorrow, but I'm flexible. I can work anywhere."

"I will need you to sign some papers to allow me to purchase on your behalf. Can you wait until I have those prepared?"

Paul stood to leave and said, "Sure. No problem."

Rich escorted him to the door and said, "I will be in touch, Mr. Smith."

Paul said, "Thank you," and left.

Rich went back into his office, closed the door, and burst into laughter. This was going to be fun. Candy Cotton won't see this guy coming. She has met her match.

Chapter 4

Rich Hayes pulled the template up on the computer and wasted no time putting together the legal papers he needed to act on Paul's behalf. When the paperwork was finished, he called the realtor handling the property. He arranged to see the building that afternoon and sent a message to Paul letting him know.

Paul went back to his hotel to work and to wait for the video that would be coming later that afternoon. He felt good about his decision to buy the property. With an apartment in town, he could come and go as he wished without checking to see if Chip had time for a visit. Also, it had no yard to keep up, which was an added convenience.

Paul sighed and faced reality. Candy was the primary reason he was doing this. The apartment was secondary. Paul pulled every fascinating part of the woman into his mind's eye. She was going to be complex and trouble, but worth the effort.

Rich met the realtor, Angie Parker, in front of the building at two o'clock. Angie had contacted Candy to let her know she would be showing the property and at what time. Rich held the door, and the two walked into the café. Candy saw them and met them halfway to the counter.

"Hello, Angie. Rich? Are you the one buying the building?" she asked.

"No," Rich replied. "But if my client is happy with the property, I will be acting on his behalf."

"His? So, your client is a man?" Candy asked.

"Yes." Rich replied. "He's from out of town, saw the property on the web, and contacted me pretty much the same way. I agreed to take his request."

Candy looked at Rich with slight confusion written on her face.

"So, you're saying that an absentee landlord from somewhere else in the country is interested in this building? Sight unseen?"

"Not quite sight unseen, Candy." Rich held up his phone.

"I am to take a video of everything and send it to him."

Rich began to video the long narrow part of the café as well as a smaller dining room to the side. Then he handed the phone to Candy.

"Would you mind videoing your kitchen? I am sure the health department would rather we stayed out of there."

Candy took the phone.

"Sure. And thanks for being understanding about that."

Candy finished making the video and returned the phone to Rich.

Angie said, "You know about the upstairs floor, but there is also a basement. We can go down there next."

Rich continued to video every inch of the basement, the back entrance, and the stairways to the left of the door. He was surprised at how large the second floor was. It covered the whole café which had been divided into different areas. He thought Paul was going to like this. It was a blank canvas just waiting for someone to paint a new look on it.

Finally, Angie showed him the small attic space. Rich climbed up and took the pictures. He stood straight up in the area. It could be used for storage or made into a loft. Rich asked the usual questions about updates to the electrical system, plumbing, and the roof. He asked if the basement was tight or if it leaked.

Rich turned to Candy and asked, "Do you want to continue renting your space, or do you have plans to move?"

"I would like to stay here if the rent is affordable. I don't know what a new owner will demand."

Rich asked, and she told him what her monthly rent was at present.

Rich said, "I think the buyer is more interested in the space upstairs. He knows you're a reliable tenant if you have been here for several years. I doubt he will want to lose you. He has plans to renovate the upstairs into an apartment for rental income."

After thanking Angie and Candy for the tour, Rich went to his car. He called his assistant to let her know he would not be back in the office and drove home. In his home office, Rich called Paul to let him know that he had the video and that he was going to email it to him. Within a few minutes the multiple videos had been sent to Paul.

While waiting for Paul to call him with a decision, Rich changed into casual clothes and took care of some minor housekeeping chores. He appreciated the stress Candy was feeling about the building being sold and was glad he could reassure her that the potential buyer hoped she would stay. An hour later, Paul called.

Seeing Paul's name on the caller ID, Rich answered, "Hello, Mr. Smith."

Paul chuckled. "Keeping in line with the ruse? Well, OK. I want to buy the building, and I will give the sellers their asking price. I don't want anyone to outbid me on this."

"Alright. I'll let the realtor know. I should have an answer for you by early evening. It depends on how long it takes Angie to get in contact with the sellers. I must tell

21

you that Candy was very nervous about my viewing the property, but she was relieved when I told her my client hoped she would stay since she seemed to be a reliable tenant." Rich then told Paul what Candy paid in monthly rent.

Paul asked, "Is it me, or does that seem a little high for a small town like Whitlow?"

"I would agree," Rich said, "but it doesn't seem to worry Candy. It's a good property, and she has a good business."

"I definitely won't raise the rent," Paul said. "I guess I'll have to take Chip into my confidence since I want him to do the renovations. What do you think, Rich?"

"I can try to handle that, too," Rich replied, "as long as you get to make the decisions for the layout and appliances. But it would be much easier to just let Chip in on your plan."

"Yeah. Well, I have time to think about that. I need to buy the place first," Paul said.

Rich replied, "Yes. Let me get off the phone and call Angie. I'll let you know the outcome later."

"Thanks," Paul said and ended the call.

A few hours later, the buyers accepted Paul's offer, and Paul drove to Rich's home to sign the necessary paperwork. Tomorrow, he would drive back to Philadelphia where he would have the money for the property wired to Rich. Paul smiled. This had been easier than he thought it would be.

Three weeks later, Paul owned the café building. The deed had been registered, insurance acquired, and the taxes paid for the rest of the year. With everything completed, Paul called Chip.

Chip answered, "Hey, bro. How are ya?"

Paul laughed, "I'm good, but did you know you are beginning to sound like a southerner? That accent is wearing off on you."

Chip chuckled, "Good. The better the accent, the better my customers feel about me. It's a crazy thing down here. Give people a southern drawl and they suddenly relax and begin to trust you."

"Speaking of customers," Paul said, "how's your business? Is it still growing?"

"It's nothing to write home about, but it's getting steady. I just got a new job this week," Chip said.

"Good. Are you building a house?"

"No," Chip answered. "Get this, the building Candy Cotton rents for her café has been sold. The new owner wants the second floor renovated to an apartment for more rental income."

"Really? What does it look like?"

Chip said, "It's a blank slate. Only load bearing beams and supports are in the space. It has an attic that could be used as a loft. It could be a really neat place to live."

"If I came down there, could I see it?" Paul asked.

"I guess so, but why?"

"Chip, you're my only family now that our parents are gone. If I have an apartment there, I can come and go without making sure you will be home or have time to hang out. My business has grown beyond just Philadelphia. I can work from anywhere that has internet and cell phone coverage. Besides, there would be no yard to worry about."

"I get that," Chip said. "To be honest, I would like to have you around, too. Philly is too far for a day trip."

Paul asked, "How's Candy dealing with her place of business being sold?"

Chip answered, "At first, she was stressed about it, but then she found out the new owner wanted her to stay and was not going to raise her rent. She's relieved about it now."

"Good. The woman can't stand me, but I wouldn't wish her bad luck."

Chip laughed. "That's hard for you to believe, isn't it. Have you ever met a woman who didn't flirt with you or try to get you to ask her out?"

"Not that I can remember," Paul said. "I'm not saying that to be cocky, but it happens. I'm not into shallow relationships. I want something lasting like you and Megan have."

"Wise man," Chip said. "So, do you really want to come and look at the apartment? Rich Hayes is handling everything for the new owner, but I'm sure he would let you see the place."

"Yes. I'll be down in a couple of days. If I'm going to rent it, maybe I can ask Rich to pass along my ideas."

"Do you want to stay with Megan and me?" Chip asked.

"No. I don't want to intrude on newlyweds. Besides, you know me, I like my space."

"Understood. Just call me when you get into town. You can at least have a few meals with us."

Paul replied, "Now that I will not pass up. See you in a couple of days."

Paul and Chip ended the call.

Chapter 5

C hip met Megan at the café for lunch. When they had received their drinks, Candy came over and sat beside Megan.

"Hey, guys. How are you?" she asked.

Megan smiled, "We're good. How are you?"

"Fine. Business is good, and the new landlord wants me to stay. What could be better?"

Chip said, "Rich has hired me to renovate the upstairs into an apartment."

"I heard that might happen," Candy said.

Chip looked at Candy and Megan then said, "You will never believe who is interested in renting it."

"Who?" Candy asked.

"Paul."

"Paul!" Candy exclaimed in a disgusted tone with a sour expression on her face. "Why? Doesn't he live in Philadelphia?"

Chip was taken aback by Candy's attitude toward Paul. He looked at Megan who also looked surprised.

He said, "Candy, you need to understand that Paul and

I are close. We are the only family we have left, besides Megan, and he wants to have a place so he can come for visits, work and not have to bother us."

Megan began to object to the last part, but Chip said, "His words, Megan, not mine. He's always been quiet and needs his own space."

"Quiet? Paul?" Candy asked incredulously. "Are we talking about the same man?"

Chip nodded yes and said, "He can be social, but he's more of an introvert. You'll never know he's up there except that you will see his car parked in the back."

Candy got a disgusted look on her face.

"No offense, Chip, but your brother and I did not exactly hit it off at your wedding. I don't care if he is an introvert, I don't want him living up there."

Chip tried to not take offense, but it was hard.

"Candy, he's a nice guy. You don't have to like him, but you can't control who rents up there. At least you wouldn't have to be afraid of a strange tenant."

Candy rolled her eyes. "Depends on your definition of strange, but I see your point."

"Anyway," Chip continued, "He's coming back into town in a couple of days to see the place. If he likes it, he will talk to Rich about renting it."

"Who owns it?" Megan asked.

"Some property company from Pennsylvania," Chip answered. "This is evidently just one of a multitude of rental properties owned by the corporation."

Candy turned up her nose. "Great. How am I supposed to contact a landlord if I don't know who to call?"

"Call me or Rich for the time being. It'll all work out," Chip told her.

"I hope you're right," Candy answered then stood because their food had arrived.

Candy walked behind the counter, made a small soft drink for herself and went to her office. She felt nauseous. Paul Garner was possibly moving in upstairs. What else could go wrong?

Paul checked into the motel in Whitlow. When he got to his room and saw that it was not too late, he called Chip.

Chip answered, "Hey, Paul. Did you get in?"

"Yes. I just checked into the motel and wanted to let you know I'm here,"

"Thanks for calling," Chip replied. "How about coming over here in the morning. I have a key and Rich's permission to show you the apartment. Jacob said he could meet us there too. He and I are going to develop a plan for the place, but you can weigh in on that since you want to live there."

"OK. I'll be at your place by nine. See you then," Paul said.

"Sounds good." Chip replied and ended the call.

Paul checked his emails then laid his phone on the nightstand and got ready for bed. It had been a long day.

Paul knocked on Chip's door at nine the next morning.

"Prompt as ever," Chip said as he let him inside the house.

Looking around, Paul said, "Nice place. Was this Megan's before the wedding?"

"Yes. It's a family home she rents from her parents. I think her grandparents lived here." Chip took his keys off a hook near the door and said, "Ready to go? Jacob is meeting us there in fifteen minutes."

"Sure," Paul replied. "I'll follow you."

Chip and Paul drove into downtown Whitlow and parked behind the café's building. Jacob met them, and the three men went through the back door and up the side staircase into the second floor. They walked into a very large open space.

"You were right when you said it was a blank canvas," Paul said to Chip. "This can easily be an apartment with two bedrooms and two bathrooms."

Paul listened to Chip and Jacob throwing out ideas for the placement of the kitchen, bathrooms, and laundry room.

Paul asked, "Does this building have access to natural gas?"

Chip answered, "Yes. Candy cooks and heats with it."

Jacob said, "I had planned to work with the gas company to have a second meter put in place for this floor."

Paul said, "Then I would put gas logs in the living area."

Before long the men had several different ideas that could work.

Chip said, "I will put together several plans with pricing and submit them to Rich. As soon as the owner decides, we can get started."

Chip looked at his watch. It was almost noon.

"How about lunch downstairs? I'm getting hungry." Jacob and Paul agreed, and the men walked down the stairs and into the café.

Soon after the three had placed their orders, Candy came by the booth.

"Hey, guys. Been upstairs developing a plan?"

"As a matter of fact, we have," Chip said. "I think it's going to be a great place to live by the time Jacob and I are finished."

Candy looked at Paul, "Is it true that you're going to rent it?"

"I want to, but I haven't signed any leases yet. I need to talk with Rich about that," Paul answered.

Candy gave a strained smile and said, "Well, I'm sure you will like living near your brother." She asked about Megan and Allie then left the table.

"Frosty," Chip said. "What did you do to her to make her dislike you?"

"I was born," Paul said sarcastically.

Jacob laughed. "I don't think I've ever seen Candy take a dislike to anyone before. Why are you so lucky?"

"I have no idea," Paul answered. "She took one look at me at Chip's wedding and decided I was an undesirable person. Maybe she will get used to my being upstairs, and we can at least be cordial. That back entrance isn't exactly private. We're bound to run into each other."

When the three men had finished eating, Chip said, "Guys, it's been fun, but I have plans and bids to put together." The men paid their bills and left the café.

The next afternoon Rich called Paul to let him know that Chip had brought by several different plans that ranged from economical to high end. Paul agreed to meet Rich at his home after business hours.

Rich laid the plans out on his dining room table. While Paul had discussed the plans with Chip, it was the first time Rich had seen them. Paul took his time and gave Rich ample time to study the suggestions and finances.

Finally, Rich asked, "Do you know which one you want?"

"They're all good. Chip does a great job, but I'm going to throw him a curve that will make him dizzy," Paul said with a laugh.

He picked the general layout he wanted then chose the room plans from two different sets of suggestions. Finally, he upgraded the appliances and fixtures in the kitchen and bathrooms.

"You're putting a lot of money into a rental," Rich said.

"Maybe, but before it's a true rental, it's going to be my home. It still doesn't have the most expensive appliances, flooring or tiles, but it's what I want to live with for now."

Paul stood and said, "Thanks for handling this, Rich. I'm assuming I have a billing statement in my future. You can give it to me any time. I'll make sure you get paid before I go back to Philadelphia."

He paused, grinned, and said, "Let me know how hard Chip's head spins when you tell him what I want."

Rich laughed, shook his head and said, "brothers," as he watched Paul leave. With a snap of his fingers, he realized that he had forgotten to ask how Candy was taking his moving in upstairs. He would have to remember to ask either Chip or Paul that question tomorrow.

Chapter 6

F inal plans for the renovations were completed, and Paul sent a down payment through Rich to help Chip get started. The most difficult part of the whole project was trying to work upstairs at times when there were few to no customers in the café. There was no way to soften the sounds of hammers and saws.

Paul rented a post office box for his company before traveling back to Philadelphia. He had decided to make the move permanent. He made all the necessary preparations, applied for a business license in North Carolina, and began deciding what household items he would take with him.

On a trip back to Whitlow, Paul climbed the stairs to the apartment to check on how the construction was coming along. He found Chip applying wallboard compound to the seams between panels of sheetrock. Paul announced himself then gave a low, appreciative whistle.

"You move fast, little brother. I never expected to see this much progress."

Chip took the compliment with a smile.

"Go look at the bathrooms. I had some of the fixtures placed before the walls went up. I think you'll appreciate it."

Paul looked in the master bath. A long, two sink vanity lined one wall. A large tub sat under a skylight, and the shower at the end of the room could hold two people. Paul returned to the hallway where Chip worked.

"That looks awesome, Chip. You should hold an open house before I move in. People need to see what you can do."

Chip watched Paul inspect every room.

He chuckled, "Paul, you inspect the place like you own it. I don't think the property company has even called to ask how things are going."

Chip stopped abruptly, his putty spatula in midair.

Suddenly it all made sense, and he looked at Paul and said, "You're the owner. You're the one who bought the place."

Paul grinned and looked at Chip. He said, "Guilty. But please keep this to yourself. You can't even tell Jacob. I'd rather you didn't tell Megan, but I won't make you keep secrets from your wife. Just tell her to keep it confidential."

"Why? Why buy it at all, and why keep it a secret?" Chip asked.

"My reason for wanting an apartment here was completely honest and the primary reason for buying it. I'm not sure I can explain the second reason, but I was in here the day Candy found out the building was up for sale. She was visibly upset. I know she doesn't like me, but she's good friends with your wife and Allie. I could afford the place, and it just seemed like the thing to do at the time."

"Do you own the property company, too?"

"Yes. I own the property company along with Garner Logistics. I've been collecting rental properties for a few years now. At first, they were just good deals I accidently ran across, but now I search them out. My friends, Ted and Cathy, run the company for me. All I do is buy the places and occasionally get a profit check. Most of the rents go back into the business for repairs when renters move out. I put this place in the company name because the café really is rental property."

"I won't tell anyone," Chip assured him. "I will tell Megan, though, but I promise she will keep it confidential. Please let me be around when Candy finds out you're her landlord. Whitlow will need a license for the fireworks that will erupt at that moment. That woman will have smoke coming out of her ears!"

Paul laughed, "I know. I may be digging my hole deeper by keeping silent about owning the building, but I keep my business dealings private. I always have."

Paul looked at his watch.

"It's close to lunch. Want to take a break and eat downstairs? I need to support my renter," he said with a grin.

"Sure. Go get a table. It'll take me a few minutes to clean up here."

35

Paul went back down the stairs and entered the café from the rear employee entrance. Candy was startled to see someone coming in that way until she recognized Paul and watched him take a table. She groaned inwardly, knowing she would have to get used to his possibly coming in that way. Candy didn't realize her attitude was different when Chip did the very same thing.

Candy rolled her eyes in disgust. How did Paul happen to take a seat in her area?

When Chip had joined Paul, she walked over, looked at Chip and said, "Hey Chip. How are you? How's Megan?"

"We're fine," Chip said and gave her his order.

Candy turned to Paul and with a slight frost in her voice she said, "Back in town, I see. What brings you this time?"

"Hello to you, too, Candy. I hope you are well," Paul replied and gave her his order without answering her question.

Candy took the orders, turned, and left the booth with no further conversation.

Chip looked at Paul with amazement, "Whatever did you do to her? I have never seen her rude to a customer, but she was rude!"

Paul shook his head, "I'm telling you, Chip, I haven't done anything to her except escort her out of the church at your wedding. She took one look at me and decided to dislike me."

Chip whispered, "She is going to explode on you when she finds out your secret."

Paul grinned, "I know. I can't decide if I want that to happen sooner or later. Both have advantages and disadvantages."

"You're a glutton for punishment, but I think I would give her a few months of an attentive landlord who keeps his hands out of her business."

"Speaking of attentive landlord," Paul said, "at some point I would like you to ask her, on behalf of the landlord, if anything needs repairing. It would be better to get those out of the way before she finds out who the owner is. Surely there are problems that older couple didn't want to deal with."

Chip nodded in understanding. "Probably. I'll ask her when you aren't around."

Candy brought their food, said, "Enjoy," and retreated to the kitchen.

When they were finished eating, Paul paid the bill for both meals and left. Chip sat a while longer finishing his soft drink.

Candy came over and asked, "Do you need anything else, Chip?"

"Chip pointed to the bench opposite him and said, "Sit for a minute, Candy."

Candy looked surprised but did as he asked.

Chip asked, "Have I done something to make you angry?"

Candy looked surprised and said, "No! Not at all, why do you ask?"

"You just seemed angry when I came in for lunch. If you aren't mad at me, then I assume Paul did or said something to make you angry. You were pretty frosty with us, and that's totally unlike you. I just want to clear the air."

Candy looked chagrined. "I'm sorry, Chip. I never meant to seem rude or angry. You have done nothing to deserve that."

"But Paul has?" he asked.

Candy looked thoughtful, "I, uh," she stammered. "Chip, I'm sorry, but I just don't like your brother. Every time I'm around him it feels like my nerve endings go raw, and I don't like that feeling. He seems to set off everything bad in my personality."

"Well, I can't help you there," Chip said. "He's going to live upstairs. It's official. I suggest you find a way to make peace with yourself in his presence because you will be running into him. A lot."

Candy sighed, "You're right. I'll try to be less abrasive around him, but, Chip, it's hard. I just want to snarl at him."

Chip chuckled, "Claws in, girl. You can manage." Chip left a tip and went back upstairs to work on the apartment.

Chapter 7

O ver the next three months, Paul made frequent trips from Philadelphia to Whitlow, checking on the progress of the apartment. Finally, Paul got the phone call he was hoping for.

"Good news," Chip said. "You can set a moving date. Everything has passed inspection. I just have a few cosmetic things to repair, and I'm done."

"That's really good news," Paul replied smiling. "I've already packed the things that I want to bring down. I'll get them delivered."

"What are you going to do with your place in Philly?" Chip asked. "It's a nice condo."

"I'm thinking about selling it. It would be a good rental, but the Homeowners' Association dues would offset any profit. I'm not rushing into anything."

"That's probably wise," agreed Chip. "I do have something to talk to you about. I'm going to send you some pictures. I asked Candy about problems in the café. There are some issues that if they aren't corrected could eventually affect her sanitation grade."

"Ok," Paul replied. "Send the pictures. I'd like to see what the previous owners didn't want to repair."

"Sending now," Chip said.

Paul looked at the photos Chip sent.

"Whoa," Paul said. "You weren't kidding. I'm surprised the health department hasn't cited her with these structural issues. I would bet money that this is why the owners wanted to sell. Go ahead and fix whatever she needs. She may have to close a couple of days to take care of everything. If she does, see if anything else needs remodeling or updated. We may as well take care of it all at the same time."

"OK," Chip said. "I'll let you know what and how much before I start. But I have to say, you're going to a whole lot of effort to please a woman who doesn't like you."

Paul sighed, "I know. Believe me, I'm not sure I understand why. Nothing I do would impress her, but since I own the building, I want it to be a quality rental."

"And you still don't want anyone to know you own the place?" Chip asked.

"Technically, Blue Ridge Properties owns the building. I just happen to own Blue Ridge Properties. So, if anyone asks, give them the company name," Paul replied.

"Alright," Chip answered. "I better go. Let me know when you're going to move in."

"I may call the furniture company to deliver what I bought. Would you meet them and let them in?" asked Paul.

"Sure. Just let me know when."

"Thanks, Chip," Paul said. "Do anything you want to market your company before I move in. Pictures, open house, I don't care. Make it work for you."

"I'll probably just take photos. The finished product is incredible. Take care. See you soon," Chip said and ended the call.

Candy had started the day annoyed, but now she was furious. All morning long a furniture company from Winston Salem had been going up and down the stairs to Paul's apartment delivering and setting up furniture. The back entrance had been blocked so many times that some of her employees had to park on Main Street and come in through the front door.

Late in the afternoon, Candy heard yet another person walking heavily up the stairs. She opened the kitchen door to the back entry area to see Paul placing a large box at the bottom of the stairs then go back to his car. When he returned carrying another box, Candy pounced.

"Do you have any idea how noisy, intrusive, and annoying these deliveries have been all day?" she asked impatiently. "My employees were forced to park on the street and come in through the front door because the entire back entrance was blocked. Customers sitting in booths near the back complained about the noise. I want to know when this will be finished, and I can get my café back to normal."

Paul was tired. He had left Philadelphia before dawn and was trying to get his clothes and personal items into the apartment. He still needed to go shopping for food and incidental household items like towels and linens because there were no sheets on the bed that had been delivered.

Paul felt his patience with Candy slip.

"Candy," he said, "I will have to see what is here before I can answer you. Right now, I am tired, I am hungry, and I just want to get this stuff upstairs before I go shopping again."

"So, you aren't going to give me an answer," Candy snapped back at Paul.

Paul placed his box on the steps and turned to Candy.

"Look, it was never my intention to inconvenience you. But I can't answer your question until I get upstairs and determine what else needs to come in."

"Unbelievable!" she exclaimed. "Is this what I have to look forward to with you living upstairs?"

"Better than sharing space with a shrew," Paul mumbled to himself.

"What did you say?" demanded Candy, her voice getting louder.

"Leave it alone, Candy," Paul said wearily. "It's almost over."

"You are so frustrating!" Candy yelled. "How am I supposed to deal with this?"

"You're not so easy to live with either," Paul replied, "but at least I'm not the one screaming. Your customers can hear you in the café, Candy. Heck, they can hear you down the street at the newspaper office. They'll probably have a reporter here in a few minutes to cover the commotion."

Candy narrowed her eyes, looked at Paul, and said in a lower, clipped voice, "Keep my back entrance clear. Have I made myself understood? If you persist in impeding my employees' ability to get to work, I will file a complaint with the landlord."

"Go ahead," Paul said. "I will just file a counter complaint against the shrew working downstairs."

"Shrew!" Candy exclaimed. "You have some nerve calling me that. You're the one at fault here, not me."

Paul shook his head, picked up his box and started up the stairs.

"I'm not dealing with this anymore," he said. "When you can be rational, then we can talk."

Paul opened the door to his apartment, went inside then closed it to block out the sound of Candy's insults. This was the first time he regretted buying the building and helping her out. He guessed it was like that saying, no good deed goes unpunished.

Paul made the last trip up the stairs with his purchases. At least for now he had the basics. He could take his time getting the rest of the items that would make his new home comfortable. Paul felt his stomach growl for the third time in ten minutes. He needed food, but he was too tired to cook. Instead, he took a deep breath and walked back downstairs and through the back entrance into the café.

Sitting down on a stool at the counter, Paul reached for a menu.

"What can I get for you?" a waitress asked.

Paul looked up. The woman was older than the high school and college students that usually worked in the evenings. Her name badge said she was Tracy.

"I need comfort food," Paul replied. "How about a hamburger all the way, a large order of fries, a large, iced tea with lemon and make it to-go."

Tracy smiled and said, "You got it. I'll be right back with your drink."

Paul put the menu back and stared briefly at the television on the wall. The evening news was on, but he was too tired to pay attention. Tracy brought his drink and placed it on the counter in front of him.

"You're the guy who moved in upstairs today, aren't you?" she asked, then said, "I'm Tracy."

"I'm Paul, and yes, I moved in. How did you know?"

"The back door was open when Candy was yelling at you. I got a glimpse of you trying to edge your way up the stairs. I had no idea she could be so unreasonable. She's the epitome of patience and understanding with all of us who work here."

Paul snorted a laugh.

"Lucky me. I guess I just bring out her worst qualities, but I'm glad she doesn't treat her employees that way. That says good things about her. Maybe she will soften toward me. If not, it isn't going to be a pleasant experience living up there."

Tracy smiled, "Just avoid her. That shouldn't be a problem once you've moved in completely. I have to say, your apartment turned out beautifully. Chip let me look at it last week just as he was finishing."

"Yes, I like the final product," Paul replied, but before he could say anything else Candy put his order in front of him.

"Here's your order. And if you don't mind, I would appreciate you not bothering my staff," she said curtly.

Looking around, Paul could see he was one of two customers left in the diner. He rolled his eyes and shook his head.

Handing Tracy several bills for the check he said, "Keep the change, Tracy. Thanks for the conversation. Have a nice evening."

Ignoring Candy, Paul took his meal and retraced his steps to the apartment.

Downstairs, Tracy said, "Candy, what was that about? He wasn't doing anything wrong. You always tell us to get to know the customers so they'll come back. Why are you so mean to him?"

Candy looked at Tracy and said, "I do not like that man. I wish he wasn't living upstairs, and I wish he just wouldn't come into the café."

"What did he do to you?" Tracy asked.

Candy gave Tracy a blank look. "Do I need an excuse to like or dislike someone? I don't think so."

Tracy said, "Well, I hope he comes in here a lot. He's a nice guy, and I want to get to know him."

"Fine. But you'll see. You'll end up not liking him, either."

"I doubt that," Tracy said, "I already like him too much to change my mind."

Candy rolled her eyes then turned to walk back to the kitchen. Somewhere in the back of her mind rose a small bit of conscience that wondered if she had indeed taken things too far. Candy involuntarily shook her head to rid herself of that thought process.

Originally, there had been an aluminum awning over

the café entrance. Paul had it removed, and a small balcony was built along the entire width of the building. This gave Candy a much sturdier awning and gave him a place to sit outside. Paul retreated there and ate his burger and fries. He was tired and distressed. He had bought this building with such good intentions, but today he regretted his purchase.

There was no way he could ever please Candy. They would never be friends. She could barely tolerate him. Well, he would live here, for a while at least, and keep out of her way. Eating at the café would be convenient at times, so he would just have to get Tracy to give him her schedule. At least she was a friendly face.

Chapter 8

Paul had taken for granted the exercise rooms at his Philadelphia condo and the motels he used. As a temporary solution he started rising early and running. He was returning from one of those runs when he ran into Chip outside the back entrance of the café.

"Hey," Paul said. "What are you doing here?"

"I'm doing repairs on the café," Chip said.

"How's that going?"

"We just got started. Candy has closed the café today, so I hired a few guys to help me get the work done in one day," Chip said.

"Can I see?" Paul asked.

"Sure. Follow me."

Chip led Paul into the café where they already had the lower part of one wall torn out. The floor was being leveled and the sheetrock replaced. Jacob was working on upgrades in the plumbing and drainage systems."

"Can you get all this done today?" Paul asked.

"I think so. The work will go into the evening, but it should be finished by the time Candy wants to open for breakfast. Megan made me promise Candy would be closed only one day. Why Megan is so protective of that woman is beyond me."

"Yeah. I've given up," Paul said. "I just avoid her."

Chip winced. "Sorry about that, but I don't blame you. She really is unreasonable where you're concerned. Megan didn't believe me when I told her how she had been treating you. Megan said Candy would never do that and that I must be mistaken. Then I told her how Candy had treated both of us at lunch that day. She was speechless, and Megan is rarely speechless."

Candy had gone to the café with plans to catch up on the paperwork in her office. She stopped just outside the kitchen door and listened to the conversation between Chip and Paul. Candy closed her eyes and leaned against the wall. How embarrassing. Her best friends thought she was being unreasonable where Paul was concerned. Was she? How could they judge her? And how could Paul irritate her so badly when everyone else loved him?

She sighed and slipped into her office unnoticed. The answer was that she would just avoid him. With that decision made, Candy settled behind her desk to get caught up on her paperwork.

That evening, the work was finished, and Chip was showing Candy what they had done.

"This is amazing," Candy said. "You and Jacob worked wonders. I can't wait for the next time the health department comes in and sees the changes. It should be worth at least a five-point increase in my rating. I could never get anything but the lowest A rating because of the plumbing issues and that rotten wall. Are you sure I don't have to pay for any of this?"

"Positive," Chip said. "Blue Ridge Properties is taking care of everything since it's all structural. Now, if you want the interior paint changed, I think that may be on you."

Candy laughed, "Yes, I guess it would be. But I'm happy with the décor for now. You know," she continued, "I was apprehensive when the building sold, but it has turned out to be quite a good thing for me. I have an attentive landlord who wants things to be done right, and my rent was not increased."

Candy's attitude annoyed Chip because of the way she treated Paul.

He said, "Yes. It has been good for you. Be grateful it turned out this way and it wasn't someone who would turn you out to find another home for your café."

Candy looked startled at the slightly sharp tone in Chip's voice. Had she offended him?

Feeling slightly offended herself at his tone, she replied in her own mildly sarcastic voice, "Yes, well, my lucky day. Is there anything else you need to show me?"

"No. That's all. It's late and I need to be getting home. See you later, Candy," Chip said and left the building.

Candy turned out the lights and locked the back door. On the way down the back steps, she met Paul coming in.

"Hello, Paul," she said trying to be friendly. Maybe she should try harder after the conversation she heard this morning.

Paul nodded and said, "Candy." That was all. He moved past her and entered the building.

Part of Candy was relieved that they had not gotten into another argument, but part of her was annoyed that he barely acknowledged her presence.

Over the next few weeks, Candy noticed that Paul never came in for breakfast or lunch. The only time he entered the café was in the evening when Tracy was working, and even then he got his meal to-go. Candy got the distinct impression that Paul was avoiding her. Well, that was fine with her, or was it? She'd never had anyone go to such great lengths to avoid her, and she found it irritating.

Chapter 9

Midmorning, Candy was working at the counter when she saw Paul walk through the restaurant and take a booth near the door. He wasn't dressed in his usual casual attire. Instead, he had on dark dress pants that fit his frame flawlessly. His dress shirt had the sleeves rolled up, and the top button was undone leaving his throat and a small glimpse of his collar bone exposed. Even if she didn't like the man, she could appreciate how fit and handsome he was. She noticed he was on his cell phone as he walked through the café and took a seat.

Candy watched as he ended his call then stood up. The café door opened, and a woman walked in. Candy could only gawk along with every other person in the restaurant. The woman was stunning. She was dressed in a black shift with a lightweight black jacket. A black and tan snakeskin belt and high heels were her accessories, and she carried a large leather bag.

Paul hugged the woman and motioned to her seat. They sat and talked animatedly until the waitress took their orders.

When the waitress walked by, Candy asked, "Who's that with Paul?"

The waitress answered, "He called her Tonya. That's all I know. Sorry."

"No worries. I was just curious."

"Yeah, you and every other diner in the place," the waitress replied.

Candy watched the couple while she worked. When they finished eating, Candy was surprised the woman did not leave. Instead, she walked with Paul through the café to the back. They went out the back door, and Candy could hear them going up the stairs to Paul's apartment.

Candy was stunned. She had never known Paul to take a woman upstairs, and surprisingly, she could not decipher her feelings about the incident. Part of her was neutral on the issue, but a tiny speck of jealousy was there. Where did that come from?

Thirty minutes later, the couple came back into the café. This time the woman was carrying what looked to be an expensive camera. They approached Candy.

Paul said, "Tonya, this is Candy Cotton. She owns the café and rents from the same property company that I do. Candy, this is Tonya DeBoe. Tonya writes for an interior design magazine. Her husband, Chase, is one of my best friends from college where he and I played basketball together. I told Chase about my move, he told Tonya, and Tonya wanted to see the place since it had been a completely open space."

Tonya said, "Hello, Candy. It's nice to meet you. I have permission from the property manager to take pictures of the building. Would you mind if I take a few shots of your café and include them in the article? It would be free advertisement, and I promise a few of the readers will make the pilgrimage to taste the food in a small southern café."

Candy looked at Paul who said, "She is showing every room in my apartment. It will be alright. I trust Tonya."

Candy looked at Tonya and said, "I guess it'll be OK. What kind of pictures do you want?"

Tonya said, "Just the lunch counter, the row of booths, some of the decor, and the front facade. If anyone is in the pictures, I have permission forms for them to sign so that I may publish them. I would really like one with you behind the counter."

"What do I do?" Candy asked.

"Just do what you would do if I weren't here. In fact, I'm going to stand back here for a while and take random pictures as you and your staff work."

Candy watched Tonya and Paul retreat to the back of the café and start talking. They didn't seem to be interested in her or the staff at all. Before long the lunch rush began, and Candy forgot that Paul and Tonya were still in the back of the room.

Paul approached some of the diners he had gotten to know, introduced them to Tonya and gave them release forms to sign. They gave forms to the waitresses to be signed, and then they approached Candy.

Tonya said, "Thank you, Candy. I appreciate your time and permission to do this."

She handed Candy a form.

"If you will sign this, I will put your café in the article. I'll make you the same promise I made Paul. Nothing goes to print without your seeing it first. I don't like surprises, so I don't like to surprise the people who are kind enough to let me into their homes or businesses."

Candy signed the form and handed it back to Tonya. Tonya thanked her, and Paul escorted her to the sidewalk in front of the café. Candy watched as they talked a while longer. Then they hugged, and Tonya got into her car and drove away.

Candy watched Paul look up to the balcony on the front of the building. He came inside, ordered an iced sweet tea from the cashier and started walking toward the back of the café.

As Paul walked by, he held up the tea and said, "I've gotten hooked on your tea, Candy. It's really good, especially on a hot summer day."

Candy watched in shock as he left the room. Paul had never complimented her before. What shocked her more was that it made her feel good.

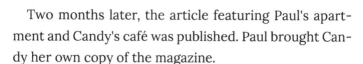

Two months later, the article featuring Paul's apartment and Candy's café was published. Paul brought Candy her own copy of the magazine.

He said, "I thought you might like to have a copy. The article turned out great. Tonya is amazing with words and a camera."

"Thanks," Candy said as she nervously took the magazine.

Paul watched her flip through the pages until she found the article.

"Oh, my," she said. "This is incredible!"

Paul smiled. Tonya had made Candy's café look like the center of a charming, small southern town. The photos featured smiling customers, hardworking staff, and Candy smiling behind the lunch counter as she took a customer's order. The core of the article was the before and after pictures of Paul's apartment. Both Candy and Chip were getting unbelievable advertisement.

The end of the article listed the café's social media page and website. Candy pulled her phone out of her pocket and checked them. She had already gotten multiple hits on both. She smiled at Paul.

"This is wonderful. Please thank Tonya for me when you talk with her again."

Paul nodded. "I called her as soon as I saw the article. She's pleased with it, and so is her editor. Their office has gotten calls asking for Chip's business information because I didn't list any. A lot of calls have been from Winston Salem. He might get some business over there."

Paul noticed that when she smiled, Candy's eyes sparked, and he could see the joy within.

Without thinking, he said, "You should smile more, Candy. You positively glow when you do."

He turned to leave and said, "Enjoy your moment of fame. Those are fleeting in life."

Candy watched Paul leave the café. He said I glow when I smile? She frowned. That was two compliments in two months. What was he up to? Or was he a nicer person than she had given him credit for being? A customer caught Candy's attention, and she soon forgot about Paul.

Chapter 10

Summer moved into autumn. Paul often spent Saturdays at Chip and Megan's house watching college football. On one of those evenings in October, the three sat around the table eating dinner.

Paul said, "You two had your first wedding anniversary, didn't you?"

Megan smiled and said, "Yes. One year. I can barely believe it's been a whole year."

Chip grinned, "The reason we invited you over is to let you know that you're going to be an uncle."

Paul let out a whoop. "No kidding? Me, an uncle? Wait, isn't Allie pregnant, too?"

Megan was all smiles, "Yes! She's about two months ahead of me. She's due in March, and I'm due in May."

Paul said, "I can't imagine a kid having any greater parents than you two. Congratulations."

Chip said, "Thanks. We're extremely happy and excited."

"Well, I can't wait to see what wonders you perform on the kid's nursery," Paul said. "Will you have time to even work on it? You got a boatload of work from Tonya's article in that magazine."

Chip grinned, "Yes, I'm booked out until after Christmas, but I keep the weekends free. We have the plans for what we want, so it will be ready in plenty of time."

Paul grinned, "Me, an uncle." He looked at Chip and Megan and said, "You know it's my right to spoil the kid rotten."

Chip looked at Paul and said, "I wouldn't expect anything else, Bro."

Paul had gotten into the routine of going into the café in the middle of the morning and ordering a large, iced tea. He kept to his routine, but this time he was smiling to himself.

"What has you in such a good mood?" Candy asked as she handed him the tea.

Paul stopped for a moment and thought. They had not told him to keep it a secret, and Megan's parents already knew.

Paul smiled and said, "I'm going to be an uncle!"

"What?" Candy exclaimed. "Megan's pregnant?"

"Yep. They told me at dinner Saturday night. I promised to spoil the kid rotten."

Candy smiled, "That's wonderful. No wonder you're smiling. I'm happy for them. When's Megan due?"

"She said May. They're all excited because Allie is due in March, and their babies will be the same age." Paul frowned and asked, "What kind of gift do you get new babies?"

Candy laughed, "I guess you don't get invited to many baby showers, do you?"

"I guess not. What's a baby shower?"

"It's just a party the girls give each other where everyone who comes brings a baby gift."

"No, I definitely have not been to one of those, and I don't intend to go to one. I'll wait until they tell me the gender, then I'll decide what to get. It's important that we favorite uncles get just the right thing," he said with a grin.

"Favorite uncle?" Candy asked sarcastically. "Don't you mean only uncle?"

Paul laughed. "True, but I like favorite uncle. It has a certain ring to it, doesn't it?"

Candy laughed. "Whatever, only uncle. As only uncle you can call yourself whatever you want. But the rest of us know the truth, only uncle."

Paul laughed, "I'm crushed. Let me bask in the glow of favorite uncle status for a little while, at least."

Candy laughed harder, "OK favorite only uncle, it is."

Paul squinted, pointed to Candy and said, "You wait. The kid's gonna love me."

Candy laughed even harder, "Of course. You're the favorite only uncle."

Paul watched Candy laugh and realized she was pretty when she wasn't frowning.

Candy stopped laughing and asked, "What is it?"

Paul sighed. "I think that's the first time I have ever heard you laugh. It's nice."

He raised the tea and said, "Thanks. I'll see you later."

He left Candy staring with her mouth open. It was the first time he heard her laugh? That's ridiculous. She laughed all the time.

Chapter 11

Paul sat on his balcony and watched the children dressed in Halloween costumes going from store to store collecting candy. He was tired. He had driven all day to get back from Florida. He had been there several days to formalize agreements with new customers. His business now extended from Maine to Miami, Chicago to New Orleans, and every possible combination in between. He was busier than he had ever been. The business was lucrative, but he had little time to enjoy the profits. He needed an assistant.

As it grew dark and the children ceased to be on the streets, Paul went downstairs to order a meal. He was relieved to see Tracy working the counter. Grabbing a menu, Paul sat on the stool at the end of the room near the back door.

"Are you sneaking in tonight?" Tracy asked.

"No. Just too tired to walk any farther," Paul replied.

"You've been out of town, haven't you?" she asked.

"Yes. How did you know?"

Tracy smiled, "You haven't been in to order tea in three

days."

"Miss Tracy, are you keeping tabs on me?" Paul asked with a grin.

"Well, someone's got to. I don't see anyone else stepping up to care if you come in out of the rain or not," Tracy said.

Paul dropped his head then looked up, "I guess you're right. Thanks for caring, Tracy. I appreciate it. It used to be Chip and me, but now he has Megan. Don't get me wrong. I'm happy for him, and things are as they should be. But you're right. Plus I am a bit of a loner, so I guess that complicates the situation."

Tracy turned to give his order to the kitchen. The café was quiet. Most people in town went to the Methodist Church for hotdogs on Halloween. Tracy was the only waitress in the restaurant.

"Candy left you minding the store, didn't she?"

Tracy shrugged, "It's alright. I do this for her every Halloween so she can give out candy and volunteer at the church. You'll be the last customer tonight. I will just twiddle my thumbs until closing."

Tracy gave Paul his food then went to the close the other dining room.

She came back and said, "Well, that's done. Now I just have this area to clean and then I can go home."

"Where's home, Tracy?" Paul asked.

"I live in Troy, the next town over. I've worked here long enough that Candy trusts me to manage things when she's gone. I've done this type of work since I was sixteen. She pays the best."

"That's good." Paul pointed to the ring on her finger. "Hubby?"

"Mike. He drives a truck long distance. I schedule this job around his runs. I make sure I'm not working when he's at home."

"Makes sense. Hard to have a marriage when you never see each other," Paul said.

Neither realized Candy had entered through the back door and was standing at the entrance to her office. She listened to the two chatting like old friends. She sighed. She knew how he felt. She had no siblings, and she lived alone. Plus, all her friends were married and now some were expecting children.

Candy walked into the main dining area.

She went behind the counter and said, "Tracy, didn't you tell me Mike was getting in tonight?"

Tracy smiled, "Yes. He's coming home." She looked at her watch. "He should be there in about an hour."

Candy said, "You go on. I'll close."

Tracy grinned and said, "Thanks, Candy. I'll owe you."

"Nonsense. It's no trouble. Go on, now. Don't keep a good man waiting," she said grinning. She and Tracy shared a knowing grin, and Tracy left.

Paul and Candy watched Tracy leave.

"That was nice of you, Candy. You could have stayed at the church and just let her close the café, but she would have been here another hour or more."

Paul looked at her intently, "You came back just to do that, didn't you?"

Candy smiled, "Guess I'm busted. Tracy is my best waitress and assistant manager. I can't run this place without her. I owe her more than she will ever owe me."

Candy looked wistful.

"Besides, they have a good marriage. I hope I have one as good as theirs someday."

Paul was seeing a different side of Candy. She was extremely thoughtful and caring to her friends and employees. Paul was tired, but for some reason he didn't want the conversation with Candy to end. He was hoping it would become the norm for them instead of fighting.

"How much extra business have you had since the magazine article?"

Candy thought for a moment and said, "Only a little. Everyone around here already knew about the café. I've had a lot of inquiries online, people asking where Whitlow is. I think the town has benefitted from the article with an uptick in people passing through, stopping and shopping."

"That's good," Paul said.

Candy looked into the kitchen. "Nick, is everything clean in there?"

"All clean, Candy. Need something?" Nick asked.

"No. Close up and go home. I'm locking the door," Candy said.

Paul heard Nick say, "Fine with me. See you tomorrow, Candy."

"Goodnight, Nick," she called.

Paul watched Candy lock the front door and turn off the outside lights. She walked through and turned out the lights in the restaurant. All that was left were the lights in her office, the kitchen, and the security lights that stayed on all the time.

Paul handed Candy the money for his meal. "I guess I shut the place down." He chuckled, "I haven't done that since college."

Candy giggled, "I hope those times were later than seven in the evening."

Paul said, "A lot later. But I was a lot younger then, too. Thanks for the dinner, Candy. See you later."

Candy replied, "You're welcome. Goodnight."

Paul left the café.

Chapter 12

Paul walked up the stairs to enter his apartment but changed his mind. He decided to walk back down the stairs and sit on the furniture he had placed outside the backdoor for his and the café employees' use.

The café and back entrance were dark.

He started to open the outside door, but he heard Candy say, "I don't have any money. I don't even have a purse. Can't you see that?"

Paul opened the door a little more. Under the streetlight he could see a man in a mask threatening Candy with a gun and trying to rob her. Paul pulled out his phone and dialed 911. He whispered his location and reported that an armed robbery was in progress.

Paul saw that the man was getting ready to grab Candy. He flipped the switches that turned on every outside light on the building and rushed through the door. The robber held his hand to his eyes. Paul knocked the gun out of the man's hand and swept his feet out from under him. Once he was on the ground, Paul turned him over and pulled the man's hands behind his back.

At that moment, a city police car pulled into the parking lot with its blue lights flashing.

An officer got out and asked, "Candy, what's going on? Which one was trying to rob you?"

Candy said, "The one on the bottom, Hank. The one on top is Paul Garner. He lives upstairs."

The police officer reached down and said, "You can let go, Mr. Garner."

Paul did. The officer hauled the man to his feet and pulled the mask off his face.

"Frank Logan," he said, "You're under arrest for attempted armed robbery." After putting the man in the car, he took a plastic bag and carefully put the pistol in it.

"Thanks, Hank," Candy said. "I didn't expect any trouble. This is the first time something like this has ever happened."

Hank said, "Is this the first time you've ever closed and come out by yourself?"

Candy hesitated then said, "Yes. I guess you're right."

"I recommend you and your staff leave together. Whitlow is a great place to live, but even we have the occasional law breaker," the officer said.

"Thanks, Hank. I will put that into practice," she promised him.

Candy and Paul watched the police car drive out of the parking lot and turn toward main street. Candy sat down on the steps. She was shaking.

"Are you alright?" Paul asked.

"I'm a little shaky, but I'm fine. Thank you. What made you come outside?" she asked.

"I'm not sure. I was getting ready to go inside the apartment when I suddenly changed my mind and wanted to sit outside for a bit. I'm glad I chose the back instead of the balcony."

"I am too," Candy said. "When did you know something was wrong?"

"As soon as I started to open the door. I heard the guy talking to you. I called 911 and turned on the outside lights. Officer Hank was here in under five minutes. He must have been close by."

Candy was still trembling.

Paul said, "Come upstairs. You can't drive while you're shaking like this."

Candy stood and grabbed Paul's hand. "I've never experienced anything like this before. I had no idea I would respond this way."

Paul led her into the building and up the stairs.

"I don't think anyone knows how they will respond to an attempted robbery until they're in the middle of it. I heard you, Candy. You were pretty bold and sassy with the guy. I was impressed."

Paul opened his door and led Candy to the couch in the living area. He went behind the kitchen island and got a bottle of wine that he had opened earlier and left on the counter to breathe. He took it and two glasses to the coffee table in front of the couch.

After he poured a glass, he handed it to Candy and said, "Here. Drink this. It has just enough alcohol to calm you down." He poured himself a glass and sat back on the couch.

Neither spoke for a few minutes.

"I like your place," Candy said. "It looks better in reality than in the pictures in the magazine. It suits you."

Paul smiled, "The landlord let me help Chip design it. I may stay forever."

Candy looked around. She saw the gas logs, the balcony, the comfortable furniture.

"This is amazing. How do you even leave the place?"

"I've gotten used to it. Besides, I need to buy groceries at least once a week," he said.

"Can I see the rest of it?"

"Are you steady enough to stand?" Paul asked.

"I think so."

He said, "Come this way." He showed Candy the extra bedroom, the bathroom in the hall, and opened the door to his bedroom.

"Oh my," Candy said. "I love this."

The room had a king size bed, a sitting area with a television, a desk, and large storage cabinets. Paul walked her through the room and showed her the master bath and the two walk-in closets.

"I'm in love," Candy said. "If you ever decide to move, let me know. I want this place."

She giggled, "But the commute would be a killer."

Paul looked at her and took the empty wineglass.

"You don't drink do you?"

Candy shook her head no. "How did you know?"

Paul answered, "You've had one glass of wine and you've got a buzz."

Paul led her back to the couch and got her a glass of cold water.

"Here, drink this. Hydrate."

Candy sat back into the couch cushions. She was slightly lightheaded and very relaxed. Taking the glass of water, she drank most of it in one gulp.

"Careful," Paul said. "Don't choke."

Candy sighed. "Have you brought any dates home since you moved in?"

Paul looked at her. She was still buzzed.

"No. I haven't dated any in Whitlow." He smiled, "Why do you ask?"

"Oh, just curious. You're a handsome man, and all the single women talk about you when they come into the café," she answered.

"The single women talk about me?" he asked.

"Oh, yes. Every one of them wants you to ask them out, but they don't know how to get to know you. You're very elusive," Candy said.

"That's on purpose," Paul said. "I'm really a bit of an introvert. I don't like crowds."

"Me neither," Candy said. "I get so tired having to be social, talkative and upbeat for people. I mean, I like being that way, but I like being quiet and alone more. That's why I came back from the church early tonight. I got tired of all the people."

Paul nodded. "I understand. I would have done the same thing."

"You would?" Candy asked.

"Yes."

Candy gave a humph, "I didn't think we had anything in common. Guess I was wrong."

Paul smiled, "I guess you were."

Candy laid her head back against the cushions, she was getting sleepy.

Paul said, "I'm going to take you home. Do you have another car to drive into work in the morning?"

"No. I only have the one," Candy answered.

"OK. Come on, Miss Cotton. I'll take you home and will be back for you at five am."

Candy said, "OK. Let's go."

She stood a little too fast, became dizzy and started to stumble. Paul caught her. He held her in his arms while he steadied her.

"Think you can walk now?" he asked.

"Yes, I can walk. I can't seem to get up too fast, though. Thanks."

"You're welcome."

Paul walked down the stairs in front of Candy, afraid she would stumble again.

He helped her into his car and asked, "Where do you

live?"

Candy gave him the address, which was not far from the café.

Paul pulled into Candy's drive and said, "Give me your house key."

Candy reached into her pocket and gave him her key ring.

"Which one is it?" he asked.

Candy looked over and said, "That one."

Paul almost laughed out loud. "OK. Can you be more specific?"

"Sorry," she said. "The one with the green plastic cover on the top."

Paul found it then helped Candy out of the car. He walked with her to her front stoop. The key wouldn't unlock the door.

"This doesn't work," he said.

"It doesn't?" she asked. "It should."

"Um, could it be to another door?"

Candy laughed, "Of course. It's the kitchen door."

Paul said, "OK. Where's the kitchen door?"

"Inside the garage," Candy answered.

"How do you get inside the garage?"

"The garage opener, silly," Candy said.

"Where is the garage opener?" Paul asked, afraid he knew the answer.

"On the visor. Where else would it be?"

Paul sighed. "Would that be the sun visor in your car

which is still back at the café?"

"Oh. Yes. Sorry," Candy answered sheepishly.

"Do you have a key hidden anywhere around here?" he asked.

"Yes," Candy answered.

"Great. Where?"

"Under the mat," she said.

Paul reached under the mat at the front door. No key. "Which mat," he asked.

"The one at the kitchen door," she answered.

Paul sighed. "Get back in the car."

"Why? We're here."

"We need to go back to the café and get the garage opener from your car. Then we will come back," Paul said.

"That makes sense. Sorry," Candy said.

Paul got Candy back into the car.

He was about to pull out of the driveway when Candy said, "Why don't you just use the key my mom keeps above the windowsill."

Paul slammed on the brakes.

"What door does that open?" he asked.

"Why, the front door, of course. If I'm not home, she can't get in the back door."

"Of course not," Paul said through clenched teeth.

He backed the car into the driveway and helped Candy out of the passenger seat, again.

Paul asked, "Which windowsill?"

"The one beside the front door."

Paul felt around the sill and found the key lodged between two pieces of wood. He opened the front door and replaced the key.

"Come inside," he said to Candy.

Candy walked through the door. She was so sleepy she could barely think straight. Paul followed Candy as she walked down the hall to her bedroom. She plopped onto the bed.

"I'm so tired," she said.

"That's from your adrenaline rush subsiding and the alcohol in the wine you drank. I had no idea you would react so strongly to that combination. Sorry."

"It's OK," Candy said. "I'll just go to bed." She laid down on top of the comforter.

Paul sighed, "Sit up."

Candy did. Paul took her jacket and shoes off.

He opened the covers and said, "Now lie down." Candy did, then she sat back up.

"What's wrong?" Paul asked.

Candy started to unbutton her shirt, "I need to get this uniform off."

Paul shook his head and said, "You're alright if you can do that. Goodnight, Candy. I will be here at five. Is your alarm set?"

"It's always set," she mumbled.

Paul was about to leave the room when Candy said, "Thank you for rescuing me tonight, Paul. I was getting scared."

Paul smiled, "You're welcome, Candy. That's what friends are for."

"Are we friends now?" she asked.

"I think so," he replied.

"Good. I was getting tired of not liking you. You turned out to be too likeable."

Paul grinned. "You can be pretty likeable too, Candy. I'm glad we are finally friends. Goodnight."

"Night."

Candy forgot about changing out of her uniform, pulled the covers up and fell asleep.

Chapter 13

C andy came out to Paul's car the next morning looking fresh and rested. When she got into his car, he just looked at her.

"What?" she asked. "Is there toothpaste on my face or something?"

"No," he replied. "You look fresh, like you had a good night's sleep. I'm dragging. How did you do it?"

"I don't know. I guess I'm a morning person. Maybe you aren't."

"I don't know what I am this morning except tired. Will Officer Hank be by today to take your statement?" he asked.

"I don't know. Probably? I've never been in a crime before. I don't know how it all works. He'll talk to you too, you know."

"I figured." Paul turned onto Main Street. "You do have your keys, don't you?"

Candy held them up and jingled them. "Are these the keys in question?"

"Yes. I certainly don't mean the key wedged between

two pieces of wood in the windowsill."

Candy laughed. "I'm sorry. I know you were frustrated, but when I think back on last night and everything that happened after you gave me a glass of wine, I burst into laughter. You had to have been so annoyed with me."

Candy laughed harder. "I was a mess."

Paul started to laugh. "Yes, you were, but I was partly to blame. How was I supposed to know that one small glass of wine was enough to make you tipsy? I will never offer you alcohol again."

Paul parked near the rear door of his building. Candy was laughing so hard tears were rolling down her cheeks.

Paul smiled, "You really were funny last night. I thought I would never get you inside your house."

Candy bent double holding her stomach. "Stop! I can't laugh any more. My stomach hurts. My cheeks hurt."

A car drove up, and Hilda, the morning cook, got out. She saw Candy bent over in Paul's car and tears were streaming down her cheeks. Hilda knocked on the passenger window of the car.

"Are you OK, Candy?"

Candy opened the door. She was sniffling and smiling. "Yes, Hilda, I'm fine. I just can't stop laughing."

Hilda looked at Paul then back at Candy, "Why are you coming to work in Paul's car?"

Candy opened the back door to the building. "It's a long story, Hilda. I'll tell you when we get inside."

Paul got out and followed them into the building. Inside

the entry he turned toward the stairs.

"Have a good day, Candy."

"Thanks, Paul. I appreciate everything you did," she said as Paul started up the stairs. She turned back to see Hilda looking at her with a shocked expression.

"What?" Candy asked.

"Since when did the two of you become friends?" Hilda asked.

"Since he stopped a guy with a gun who tried to rob me last night," Candy answered as she unlocked the café.

"What!" screamed Hilda. "What happened?"

"I left by myself last night and some guy in a mask was waiting to rob me. Stupid man. He didn't even notice I had nothing on me but keys. No purse, no money. Idiot."

"And Paul stopped him?" Hilda asked.

"Yes. He was just going to sit outside for a while and saw what was happening. He called 911 then turned on all the outside lights. It blinded the robber and gave Paul a chance to tackle him. By then Hank drove up and took the guy to jail."

"That doesn't explain why you came in with Paul just now," Hilda said.

"Oh that. I was a bit shaky last night. He took me home then came and got me this morning. We need to get the breakfast prepped. We can talk later," Candy said.

Hilda wanted to argue but knew Candy was right. They had some regulars who came in at six almost every morning.

Paul was yawning and working on a schedule for his new customers when he heard a knock on his door. He opened it and saw it was Candy.

"Hey," he said. "What's up?"

"Hank is downstairs and wants to talk with you. He's in a booth in the extra dining room," she said.

"OK."

Paul closed the door and followed Candy down the stairs and into the café. The waitresses watched in confusion. First, Candy never ventured near Paul's apartment, and second, they weren't arguing. They acted like friends.

Paul sat with Officer Hank and gave him a detailed account of the robbery. When they were finished, Hank left, and Paul walked back through the café only to be stopped by the owner of the newspaper who wanted his side of the story. It seemed word had spread, and the incident behind the café was the talk of the town.

When Paul finished talking with the reporter, he walked past Candy, leaned in and whispered, "That attempted robbery seems to have been good for business."

Candy snickered. "Yeah. Who would have thought?" she whispered back.

They didn't see the waitresses stare in astonishment. The staff never thought they would see those two civil to each other, let alone friendly.

Just as he was about to go out the door, Paul turned around, went to the waitress at the counter and ordered his usual tea.

Candy looked at her and said, "I got this."

She fixed the tea, handed it to Paul and said, "On the house. You deserve it."

Paul grinned and said, "Thanks, Candy."

He picked the tea up and walked out of the café.

Chapter 14

The last of the leaves dropped off the trees as Thanksgiving neared. Whitlow's tree-lined Main Street, which had been a colorful sight, now looked drab with the bare trees.

Paul sat on the balcony watching the town employees putting up Christmas decorations. He had read the announcement in the paper that the annual Christmas Parade would be Sunday afternoon. That gave him an idea.

Paul went inside and down the stairs to the café. He plopped on his usual stool at the counter near the back. He told the waitress he wanted a cup of coffee and to talk with Candy.

Candy came out of the kitchen, fixed his coffee, and walked to the end of the counter.

"What's up?" she asked.

"Do you have any plans for Sunday?" he asked her.

"Just church. Why?"

"I have an idea. The Christmas Parade is Sunday. If I buy the supplies, will you help me fix the food for a light supper? I want to invite Chip, Megan, Jacob, Allie and the twins over, and we can all watch the parade from the balcony."

Candy smiled, "Watch the parade from the balcony? That would be fun. Yes. I'll help you. Get the food, and I'll come over after church."

Paul smiled. "Perfect. I'll call Chip and Jacob now."

Paul didn't even wait until he was back in the apartment. He called from the café. After two calls, Paul motioned for Candy to come over.

"OK. We're on. They're excited about it, too."

"What do you want to fix?" Candy asked him.

"Just a light supper. I thought a variety of sandwiches, fruit, veggies, condiments. What do you think?"

Candy took a piece of paper and wrote a list of groceries.

She handed it to Paul and said, "Get this list of food. I can make hot sandwiches so no one has to fumble through making their own."

She pointed to another set of ingredients.

"This will make a nice cheese dip to go with the bread on the list. The other ingredients will make a fruit salad. Add chips, and you should be set. You'll need to put your own list of beverages down. I don't recommend alcohol for any of the ladies."

Paul chuckled, "I guess not. What do you suggest?"

Candy thought then added some things to the list.

"This will make a great punch and it isn't too sweet. It

83

goes over well every time I make it, even with men."

Paul looked at the list.

"This looks great. You're really good at this. Have you thought about expanding into catering?"

"I have," Candy said. "But so far, I haven't been able to save enough for all of the equipment I need to purchase."

"Yeah," he said, "I bet it's a big expense upfront."

Paul paused and said, "I will have all of this by Saturday afternoon. Why don't you come up and look it over in case I need to go out and get something else."

"Sure," she said. "Just come down and get me. You know where I'll be."

Paul picked up the list, left money for his coffee, and went back upstairs.

Saturday afternoon between the lunch and dinner crowds, Paul went downstairs to get Candy.

"I have the food," he said. "Do you have time to come take a look?"

"Sure," Candy said. "It's quiet."

Candy told the waitress that she would be right back and followed Paul up the stairs.

Paul had the food laid out on the kitchen island.

Candy arranged everything by recipe and said, "This should be all you need. Just keep it refrigerated. I have the dishes for everything. I will bring those."

"Dishes," Paul said slapping himself on the forehead. "I didn't even think about serving dishes."

Candy smiled, "That's why you have me, Mr. Garner. Caterer extraordinaire. Use disposable plates, silverware, and glasses. It's just us."

The next day after church, Candy went to Paul's apartment and started cooking. When the others arrived, the aroma of good food was flowing down the stairs.

"Something smells wonderful!" Megan said.

"OK, I'm officially hungry," Chip said.

Candy said, "Most of it is ready. The hot sandwiches will be out of the oven in about five minutes. Ice is in the sink. Beverages and glasses are on the cabinet. Help yourself."

The girls made glasses of punch while Paul handed Chip and Jacob a beer.

Allie said, "Paul, this is so exciting. I can't wait to watch the parade from a balcony. It's almost like Mardi Gras in New Orleans."

The twins, who were Jacob's half siblings, were already out on the balcony inspecting the view of the street.

Megan said, "Paul, I want to see your apartment. Chip has told me so much about it. I've been dying to see the finished product now that it's furnished."

Paul said, "As you can see, this is the kitchen and living area. Down the hall is a bedroom and a bathroom. At the end of the hall is the master suite, which is my second favorite place in the apartment."

"What's your favorite?" Candy asked.

"The balcony. Who wouldn't love a balcony overlooking Main Street?"

Megan said, "Candy, Allie and I are going to look at the rest of the apartment. Want to come?"

"That's OK. I've already seen it."

Megan looked at her and asked, "You have? Even the master bedroom?"

"Yes, even that," Candy said. "Go ahead, I have to get the sandwiches out of the oven."

Paul was watching the conversation and realized that Candy had no idea how she had shocked her friends.

Megan asked, "When did you see the apartment?"

Candy answered, "The night of the robbery when Paul brought me up and got me drunk."

"Wait, What!" Megan exclaimed. She didn't know who to look at first, Candy or Paul. "Paul got you drunk?"

"Yes. Well, he didn't mean to. It was quite an accident. It had something to do with adrenaline levels dropping after a stressful event, combined with alcohol. Anyway, I got tipsy very quickly. I have never been tipsy. Did you know that?"

Megan and Allie just stared at Candy.

Candy continued, "Before I got tipsy, Paul was being nice and let me see the apartment. That's all. No big deal."

Megan said, "Oh, I think it's a very big deal. Chip's brother brings my friend up here and gets her drunk? That's a big deal."

Candy looked shocked and said, "Megan! Paul rescued me from a robber. He was just trying to calm me down. He had no idea how I would react to alcohol. Don't be mad at him. It's no one's fault. Paul took me home and put me to bed."

"Put you to bed!" exclaimed Megan. "And just how did he do that?"

"Just like I said," Candy explained. "He drove me home, unlocked the front door, helped me out of my jacket and shoes, and I went to bed. I was too sleepy to change out of my uniform. He came back to get me the next morning because my car was still here. So, you see, it's all innocent. Just be sure to check out that big tub in the master bedroom. That is a bubble bath waiting to happen."

Megan shook her head then went down the hall to inspect the rest of the apartment. Paul burst into laughter. Candy looked at him and winked. He laughed even harder.

He went over to Candy and whispered, "You were leading her along, weren't you."

"Of course. I'm not nearly as ditsy as I sometimes appear. I'm quite intelligent."

Paul chuckled and said, "I know I will never underestimate you again, ever."

Candy replied, "See, you learn fast. You must be pretty smart, too."

Paul laughed again and reached for a sandwich. "These are amazing!" he said. "How do you make a sandwich taste so good?"

"Trade secrets," Candy replied. "Key word there is secret."

Candy gave him a sweet smile and placed the sandwiches on a tray. By that time, everyone had finished their tour of the apartment and started to fill plates with food.

When everyone had eaten, Chip looked at his watch and said, "The parade should be starting." He looked at Megan and asked, "Which way down the street does it go?"

"From the Methodist Church, past the park and ends at the hardware store," she said.

The six adults and two children gathered on the balcony just as the first police cars slowly came down the street escorting the grand marshal, who was the mayor. The twins, Mandy and Michael, were so excited they could not stop pointing and shouting.

Everyone clapped for the high school band playing Christmas carols, the dance troupes and the gymnastic students. They waved at every float that went by and every beauty queen sitting on the back of a convertible. They watched student clubs from the high school driving by in pickup trucks or riding on hay wagons. At the end came Santa Clause throwing candy out to the crowd. He saw the group on the balcony and threw candy up to them.

"Thanks Santa," Candy called. Santa waved back.

Everyone came back into the apartment and sat along the sectional couch in front of the gas logs. The twins climbed the spiral staircase to the loft.

"That was the best way I have ever seen a parade," Allie said. "Thanks Paul."

Paul smiled, "I'm glad you came. This is my first time having anyone over since I moved in. I can't think of a better group."

The sun was starting to set, and the two couples gathered their coats to leave.

"We need to help you clean up," Megan said.

Paul said, "Not this time. I'll take care of it. Maybe next time."

Megan smiled and kissed Paul on the cheek. "This was fun, thanks."

Allie and Jacob agreed with how fun the afternoon had been, and everyone left except Candy. She was putting food in storage containers for Paul.

"I can do that," he said. "You must be tired. I can't tell you how much I appreciate your doing this."

Candy smiled, "Hey, you shared your balcony during a parade. That is way cooler than making a few sandwiches. Besides, these are my serving dishes."

Paul gave a sheepish grin and said, "Oh, yeah. I forgot."

Candy sighed, "Honestly, all I have to go home to is an empty house. This has been so much fun I hate for it to end."

Paul smiled, "It really has been fun." He put the food in the refrigerator. "Where did you learn to cook like this?"

"Well, I could tell you it is a natural talent, but the truth is I took a two year food science course at the community college in Wilkes County. I learned the basics, but I found I like experimenting with recipes."

"Do you bake, too? You know, cakes, cookies, pies?" he asked.

"Yes. I really like doing that. I make all the cookies, pies, and cakes in the café. The cooks follow my menu recipes, but I'm protective of my baking. I like decorating cakes, but no one ever asks for that."

"Do they know?" Paul asked.

Candy looked pensive for a moment. "Probably not."

"You should decorate a birthday cake and put it on display with a sign that you will take orders."

"That's not a bad idea," she said. "I'll give that some thought."

The kitchen was clean and the two of them sat at the island talking.

Paul asked, "If you had a catering business, what would that look like?"

Candy said, "Ultimately, I would like to have the typical catering business for setting up buffet meals. But in addition, I think it would be fun to have all the equipment for people to rent. You know, tables, chairs with the fancy covers for weddings, table cloths, plates and crystal, punch fountains, chocolate fountains. If I had the space, I would open a bakery. Then people could order what they wanted, and I would run the event business from there."

Paul looked thoughtful, "You have this all worked out. What's stopping you?"

"Cash flow. I've saved, but I have barely reached the point I could start a basic catering business."

"I get that. I'm lucky. I can work anywhere there is Wi-Fi and phone reception. I don't have to have an office, but I've been thinking of renting one. My business has grown to the point I need help."

Paul continued, "I'm working eight to twelve hours a day to keep up with the schedules. Plus, I need to make a trip to Texas. I'm getting requests from companies there to give them an example of schedules and quotes. Keeping up with the differences in charges among freight companies is getting cumbersome."

Paul winked, "You can open your bakery, and I'll rent the top floor just like here."

Candy grinned, "You're on."

"Where would you like to open the bakery?" Paul asked.

Candy smiled and said, "Come to the balcony."

Paul followed her through the sliding door. The Christmas lights gave the street a festive ambience. She pointed to an empty building across the road.

"There. That is the old bank building. It's empty and available. It would need updated electrical and plumbing and a commercial kitchen, but you should see the inside. It has the most beautiful woodwork and ornamental ceiling."

"Who owns it?" Paul asked.

"I don't know. I've never inquired because I can't afford to do it."

Paul opened the door to go back into the warm apartment.

"I understand. I hope you get your dream," he said.

Candy replied, "Thank you. That means a lot."

Candy gathered her dishes. "I really had a good time, Paul. Thank you for including me."

"You're welcome. Thank you for cooking," he replied.

Candy smiled and said, "Anytime."

Paul helped her carry the dishes to her car then watched her drive away.

Chapter 15

The first week in December, Candy was working the lunch counter. The main rush for the midday meal was over. As she was cleaning the counter, she happened to look out the door. She saw Chip Garner going into the vacant bank building across the street. If Chip, a contractor, was going in, then someone had decided to refurbish the place.

Candy didn't know why she suddenly wanted to cry. All these years she had harbored the desire to buy the building, remodel it and start a bakery and catering service. She knew she couldn't afford it but knowing someone else had taken it completely off the market burst the bubble she had been secretly hoping to release.

With a big sigh, Candy returned to work. She told herself to drop back and punt, to lower her sights and be realistic. She couldn't afford it anyway.

A few days later, Candy sat at the lunch counter rolling silverware in napkins. It was a cold, dreary, rainy day. The days were shorter, and the sun sat lower on the southern horizon, so any cloud cover darkened the day even more. However, it also made the town's Christmas lights look brighter in the daytime.

The breakfast crowd had been slim, and no one was in the café at the moment. Candy heard Paul coming through the back door. He sat on the stool beside her.

Paul bumped her shoulder with his, "Why the sad face?"

"Sorry. I was concentrating on the most difficult of tasks, rolling silverware," she said sarcastically.

Paul chuckled.

"Besides, it's a dreadfully cold and dreary day which always reduces the number of customers."

"Can you take a break?" Paul asked.

"I can, but what do you need?"

"I need you to put on your coat and gloves. I have something to show you," he said.

Candy looked at Paul with confused surprise.

"OK," she said and told one of the waitresses that she would be gone for a bit.

Candy put her coat on and said, "I'm ready. Where are we going?"

Paul grinned, "I have a surprise."

He took her hand and led her out the front door and across the street. Taking out a key, Paul opened the door to the empty building that he and Candy had discussed the afternoon of the parade.

Candy walked in. The familiar woodwork and ornate

ceiling once again spoke to her appreciation of the craftsmanship of the past and made her sad it was out of her reach.

She turned to Paul and asked, "Why are we here?"

Paul said, "I have a business proposition for you."

"You have a business proposition? What do you mean?" she asked incredulously.

Paul said, "Hear me out. You have a talent. Your culinary skills are equal to any chef working in a five-star restaurant, and I have dined in quite a few. You just tone them down for the clientele in a small town restaurant, which is good business sense. I want to go into business with you. I will be a semi silent partner."

"Semi silent?" Candy asked. "What does that mean?"

"You build the baking, catering and event businesses. I finance it until it supports itself. But semi silent means I want to see the books and help decide what equipment we can afford and when."

"I'm listening," Candy said.

"This building has a basement and two floors above this one. I want the top floor for offices for Garner Logistics. I need to get some help. The basement is dry and tight. With a little cleaning it can store anything you need for the business. You can put a commercial kitchen in the back with a large workspace for baking, decorating, whatever bakers do. The second floor is completely open and is extra space which we can grow into."

Candy listened. Her heart was beating faster, and she

started to get excited about the prospect. Then reality set in, "What's in all this for you?"

"I need an office, and I needed to start the process this fiscal year. My business has really grown, and I need the tax write-off. I get that by buying the building and starting an office.

"Chip has already started working on that. He complains about having to go up two flights of stairs with everything, so I'm in the process of getting a permit for scaffolding with lift pulleys.

"After the first of the year, we establish the bakery. That gives us a tax year to hopefully start making a profit," he continued. "What do you say? Will you start the business with me?"

Candy looked at him, "I don't know, Paul. Why are you doing this?"

Paul said, "I'm not an idiot. I'm an entrepreneur. When I see a potential business, I go for it. To me you are a sure thing. This floor is yours to design and make work. At first, people will come in out of curiosity to see the old building refurbished. Once they taste your products, see your talent with cake decorating, and find out you cater, then the rest is easy. Profit."

Candy studied Paul's face. He was serious. "This just all sounds too good to be true," she said. After a moment's thought she grinned and said, "OK. Let's do this. Show me your plans."

Paul gave a delighted whoop, extended his hand and

said, "Partners?"

Candy smiled, took his hand and said, "Partners."

With her hand already in his, he pulled her to the side stairwell and up to the top floor. Chip had already started framing in the supports and dividing walls for the different offices and bathrooms.

"What's this big hole in the side?" she asked.

Paul grimaced. "That's for the elevator. We're required to make each floor accessible to the handicapped. I don't mind that, but the cost for an elevator and engineering consultants is crazy high. Still, I don't see any other way. Jacob is researching the electrical needs and contracting with the elevator company. This means that whatever goes on the second floor needs to be a money maker."

Paul chuckled, "Maybe we need to get a dentist in there since you're selling sugary confections on the first floor."

Candy giggled. "You're bad, but that would be a good use of the space. We could also save it for a showroom. I could set up samples of venues. We could even rent out booths for people who want to sell things on consignment."

Paul looked at her, "Not bad. You can come up with good ideas yourself. What do you want to do with the main floor?"

Candy and Paul spent the rest of the morning planning, drawing out diagrams and designs, and discussing equipment.

She looked at her watch and exclaimed, "Oh my gosh,

it's lunch time. I need to get back."

Impulsively, Candy hugged Paul. "Thank you, Paul. I love this idea. I will work hard to make it profitable."

Paul was shocked. He put his arms around Candy and hugged her back. He liked the way she felt in his arms. That surprised him.

Candy released the hug, gave him a big smile, and said, "See you later."

Paul watched her leave. He noticed that her nose was red from the cold, but it made her eyes look bluer. Paul rubbed the back of his neck. First Candy had been a challenge, then an adversary, then a friend, and now a partner. But after that hug, well, he wasn't sure where that put the relationship.

Chapter 16

I t was Christmas Eve, and Candy was closing the café early. By one o'clock, the dining rooms were clean, the front door was locked, and the staff had gone home. Only the security lights were on out front. Candy sat in her office finishing up paperwork, orders, and work schedules for the first two weeks in January.

She worked accurately but slowly. While she knew she would be spending the evening and the next day with her parents, Candy was still reluctant to go home to an empty house. She had not even decorated for Christmas. Her only exposure to Christmas decorations was in the café.

Candy was about to finish and go home when she heard a knock on the door to her office. She looked up and saw Paul.

She smiled. "Hey. What are you doing here?"

Can you come upstairs when you're finished?" he asked. "I have some things to discuss with you."

"Sure. I can come now. I'm finished and was just about to leave." Candy turned off the computer and the lights, locked the back door to the café and followed Paul up the stairs.

Candy walked into the apartment. The gas logs were burning low, and Christmas music played softly in the background. There was even a small battery operated Christmas tree blinking in the middle of the dining table.

She smiled and said, "Going all out for Christmas, I see."

Paul said, "Yep. This is my nod to the holiday. Today and tomorrow, then it's back to normal."

Paul led Candy to the kitchen island where blueprints were laid out. He showed her the plans for the bakery kitchen with large counters for the work area, commercial mixers and ovens, display cases, and seating in front. He pointed to an addition on one of the side walls in the dining area.

"I thought maybe we could put a mantel and gas logs here. Chip found an old chimney behind the wall, so there would be ventilation already built in."

"I love that idea," Candy said. "I'm glad the foyer with the elevator is separate from the bakery. Then your business and the second floor can be accessed if the bakery is closed."

"I agree. Chip did well with his planning. He should have been an architect. He's brilliant. Even the architectural consultant said so. Do you agree with these plans for the first floor?"

"I do," Candy said. "How are your offices coming?" she asked.

"Good," Paul replied. "There's a lobby and a main office

in the back with a bathroom, mine of course. Then an office and a unisex bathroom between my office and the lobby. Nothing fancy, but comfortable."

Paul pulled out one more set of plans.

"What do you think of dividing the basement up with storage cabinets but leaving a big space for large items? The elevator will go down to the lower level so heavy items can be put in there."

"I like it, Candy said. "The cabinets will keep things clean and the area neater."

"That's what I thought," Paul said. "Well, that's it for the plans."

He took a pitcher from the refrigerator and poured two glasses of red punch. He handed one to Candy.

Paul held his glass up and said, "To our new business. May the new year bring big profits."

Candy smiled and touched his glass with hers. "Cheers."

Paul grinned, took her hand and led her to the couch.

Candy said, "You're up to something. I can tell. What is it?"

Paul sat Candy on the couch and handed her a red bag. In the bag were two boxes covered in Christmas wrapping paper.

Candy squinted at him and said, "Hmm, do I trust this? Is something going to jump out at me?"

Paul laughed. "No. Open them."

Candy opened the first box. In it was a keychain. The

fob was gold with a cotton boll engraved on it. On the ring were two keys. One was a skeleton key, the other a modern industrial key.

"I love the key chain, especially the cotton boll. What do the keys unlock?" she asked.

Paul replied, "The skeleton key is an original to the building. I thought you might like to have one as a memento of the past. Of course, we replaced those locks with commercial grade security locks. That is what the second key goes to. It will open the front and the back of the bakery."

Candy smiled, "Thanks, Paul. I had not gotten far enough in my head to even think about keys."

Candy opened the second box. It was a ceramic rock. She looked at Paul in confusion.

Paul said, "It opens. Put your front door key in here and place it on the ground behind a shrub or something. Your windowsill key is way too easy to find."

Candy laughed. "I perceive a theme here. I still laugh out loud at times when I think of that night. Not the robbery, but your trying to get me home."

Paul grinned, "Yeah, that was one exercise in frustration."

Candy sighed, "Thank you, Paul. This was very thoughtful." She reached over and hugged him.

Paul responded by pulling her to him on the couch. He held her and rubbed her back.

"You're welcome, Candy." He let her go and noticed

tears in her eyes. "What's wrong?"

"You're so nice to me when I've been so mean to you. I feel bad about all of that. I don't know why I thought you were such a miserable person. You're not at all. You're actually one of the nicest people I know."

Paul smiled and pulled her back into a hug.

"That's a nice compliment, thank you. Don't worry about it, Candy. There were times when I didn't like you too much, either. I'm glad we're friends and partners now." Paul let her go and watched her smile.

"I claim the first cookie that comes out of your ovens. What kind will it be?"

Candy said, "I'm thinking chocolate chip. It's a universal favorite. I, myself, am partial to almond sugar cookies. Put a little lemon or raspberry curd in the center, and you've bitten into a piece of heaven."

Paul said, "I want one of those. I like brownies with lots of pecans. But for breakfast, you can't beat a blueberry muffin."

Candy looked at Paul and said, "You're a genius."

"I know," Paul said with a grin, "but what are you talking about?"

"A line of breakfast muffins. I can put them on the menu at the café, sell them in the bakery, and see if the coffee shop at the interstate will sell some. If they catch on, we can mass produce them and see if a grocery store will add them in their bakery section."

"Now you're talking," Paul said. "Profitable businesses

come from brainstorming, discussions, and dreams. But we need to get a following first. We have plenty of time to make that happen."

Paul and Candy sat in front of the fire, sipping their punch, and talking about the future. Candy moved her head and her ponytail of blond curls draped over her left shoulder near Paul. While listening to her he absently started to play with the ends of her hair. Neither noticed the tender gesture.

Finally, Candy looked at her watch. It was almost time for dinner.

"Oh, dear," she said. "I'm supposed to have dinner with my parents and Dad's side of the family. I'm going to be late if I don't leave now."

She looked at Paul, held up the bag of gifts and said, "Thank you for this, and thank you for a very pleasant Christmas Eve. I think it will be one of my favorites."

Putting on her coat Candy asked, "Do you have plans?"

"Not tonight. Tomorrow, Chip, Megan, and I are having lunch at Jacob and Allie's. No gifts, just spending the time together. Well, the twins will have Christmas, and Rich will be there to spoil them with gifts."

Paul looked at Candy and said, "Why don't you come with me? That is, unless you have other plans."

"No, I don't have any plans after tonight. I would just be hanging out with the parents. Will the others mind me crashing their party?"

"Nope. I'll let Allie and Megan know tonight. They will

be delighted, I promise. They like you." Paul grinned, "If you make one of those famous carrot cakes, Chip and Jacob will kiss your feet."

Candy laughed, "Well, we don't want that, but I can make the cake. What time?"

Paul said, "I'll pick you up at noon. We plan to eat at one."

"OK. That will give me time to make the cake in the morning."

Paul said, "Thanks. It'll be fun. I understand Allie wants to unveil the nursery."

Paul watched Candy's face soften.

She said, "I'd like to see that. I know she's glad it's finished. She told me she's starting to get nervous about the delivery even though it's still almost three months away."

Paul threw his hands up in a blocking motion. "I don't know anything about that birthing stuff. I don't think I want to, either. That's entirely a woman's domain in my opinion. I'm shocked to see how much Chip is getting into it. I keep asking myself who is this guy and where did my brother go?"

Candy laughed. "Just wait. Some day when you have met the woman of your dreams and she is about to give you a child, you will change your mind."

"Now that's hard to believe, but I guess you're right."

Candy said, "I need to go. Thank you so much for a great afternoon. See you tomorrow."

Paul walked her to her car and said, "See you tomorrow. Merry Christmas, Candy."

"Merry Christmas, Paul," she said as she closed her door and started the engine.

Paul climbed the stairs to his apartment suddenly looking forward to the next day more than he had been. He grinned and thought, carrot cake. Pulling out his phone, he called Jacob to tell Allie about the added guest. Just as he thought, she was delighted.

Chapter 17

Paul pulled into Candy's drive at noon on Christmas Day. He rang the doorbell, and she let him inside.

"Oh, man, it smells good in here," he exclaimed.

Candy grinned as she put her coat on. She handed the cake carrier to Paul and picked up a casserole dish.

Paul said, "I assume I'm holding carrot cake, but what is in the other dish?"

"A new broccoli casserole recipe I'm trying. I decided to let this group be the test market. If everyone likes it, I will put it on the menu as a side."

"Nice," Paul said. "See, I told you that you're a good business risk, and I mean that in the best way. All new businesses have some risk. I forgot to tell you. I sent before pictures of the place to Tonya. She wants to do an article on the finished product again. She will come to town when my office is furnished and will return for the bakery's opening day."

"That's fantastic," Candy said. "I'll be sure to have the cases filled with delectable looking baked goods. I may even leave a few decorated cakes lying around."

"Wise, woman," Paul answered. "An elaborate children's birthday cake would definitely bring in the business."

"True. People buy things for their kids they may not normally purchase for themselves," she said as they drove up to the Stone's house.

Jacob had seen them and opened the door as soon as they were on the front porch. "Merry Christmas! Come in, it's freezing out here. Did you know they've changed the forecast and we could get snow this afternoon?" he said.

"That's exciting!" Candy said.

"I hadn't heard," Paul said. "But I'm glad you're all happy about it. I've seen enough snow to last a lifetime. I lived in Pennsylvania, remember?"

When they entered the kitchen area Megan asked, "Is there a carrot cake in that carrier?"

Candy grinned and said, "Yes, Ma'am. The carrot cake has arrived."

"I could kiss you," Megan said.

"What's so special about a carrot cake," Chip asked.

Megan, Allie and Rich looked at Chip with pretend shock and horror.

Rich said, "It's not just any carrot cake. It's Candy's carrot cake."

Paul said, "I have only had one piece. Every time she makes one for the café it sells out within an hour. It's amazing."

Megan said, "Yes, and we get one all to ourselves. Merry Christmas to me!" The group laughed.

The group gathered in the kitchen, and Rich said a prayer of thanks and blessing. Everyone started filling their plates from the large spread of food. Jacob had added an extra table at the end of the dining room table so they all could eat together.

Paul took a bite of the broccoli casserole and said, "Candy, you definitely need to put this on the menu. It's delicious."

Allie asked, "Are we the test market again? If so, I agree. I really like this, and I'm not a big fan of broccoli."

Candy said, "Well if Allie likes it, then it's a winner. I know how much she dislikes broccoli."

The conversation changed as everyone listened to the twins tell what they got for Christmas. Everyone admired the necklace Chip had given Megan and the sapphire ring Jacob had given Allie.

Jacob said, "When we got married, I could barely afford wedding bands. This has been a good year, and I thought Allie needed a belated engagement ring."

Chip said, "This has definitely been a good year for me as well." He and Jacob looked at Paul.

Chip continued, "We have you to thank, Paul. That piece you let Tonya do on your apartment brought us a lot of special renovation work in Winston Salem and Mt. Airy. Jacob and I have gone in together to form a company specializing in historical restorations."

Paul grinned, "That's wonderful, but you'd better hang

on to your hats. Tonya wants to do another piece on what we're doing with the old bank building. As soon as the office on the third floor is furnished, she is coming down, then coming back on the bakery's opening day."

Chip and Jacob high fived each other.

"Looks like another good year coming up," Chip said.

Paul said, "Well, Candy and I have news."

The table went silent. Everyone knew Paul and Candy had been at odds with each other, barely tolerating each other's presence.

Paul laughed, "Rich knows all about it because he has been helping us. We have all the applications to file and start a new business in January. The bakery is part of it, but we are going to have a catering business and an event planning service."

Everyone at the table was silent.

"Well, say something," Candy said. "We're excited about it."

Megan said, "I'm surprised but also, it makes sense. I think this is great."

"Me, too," Allie said.

Rich smiled as he looked around at the others. They were shocked.

He said, "I have seen their business plan, and I for one expect a great success." He raised his glass and said, "Here's to new business ventures and a profitable new year for us all."

Everyone raised their glasses and made the toast, even

the twins who didn't understand the conversation.

When the meal was over, everyone helped clean the dining room and put food away. Allie started a pot of coffee to go with the dessert that would be served later. Everyone had complained of eating too much food to immediately follow up with dessert.

Chip pulled Paul to the side and whispered, "Bro, do you know what you're doing? We're talking about Candy Cotton, the woman who can't stand you."

Paul smiled and said, "Don't worry. We've ironed out our differences. She's an amazing cook, and she has a good business head. She has already planned how to keep the café running, start a meals-to-go business as a prelude to the catering, and designed a bakery. Chip, the woman is a food business genius. I'm just the semi silent partner who is bankrolling the venture."

"Candy?" Chip asked.

"Yes, Candy," Paul said. "I predict she will be running a well known events service within a few years."

"Candy?" Chip asked.

"Stop, Chip," Paul said firmly. "Trust me, she's amazing."

"When did all of this happen?" Chip asked.

"The night of the robbery changed things for us. We decided to be friends. Then we talked after the parade. She told me her dreams about a bakery and maybe catering. I bought the building she wanted to convert and offered her the chance to do what she wanted. I saw a prime business opportunity."

Chip stared at Paul hardly able to comprehend the change that had taken place between him and Candy.

"Unbelievable," he said. "You and Candy in business together. Next thing I know you'll be telling me you're marrying her."

Paul said, "Don't get carried away, little brother. We've become friends, and I like that. Don't rain on the parade."

Chip looked chagrined, "You're right. Sorry." He paused, then said, "I forgot to tell you that the elevator will be installed the first week in January."

"Perfect," Paul said. "I'll be glad when I don't have to climb all those stairs."

Chip rolled his eyes, "Whatever. You run steps for a workout." They suddenly heard oohs and aahs coming from upstairs.

The two men followed the voices to see Allie and Jacob's nursery. No one was surprised when they saw it had been decorated in a farming motif which was perfect for the little boy they were expecting.

The afternoon sped by as the friends and family stuffed themselves on carrot cake and other desserts, drank two pots of coffee, and divided into teams for a game of Pictionary.

Candy's casserole dish was empty, and she was dividing the rest of the cake between Allie and Megan.

Paul came over, started making sad eyes and asked, "Where's my leftover cake?"

Candy laughed, "Get over it. I'll save you a piece at the café the next time I make one."

"That'll do," Paul said agreeably.

Paul and Candy got into their car and followed Chip and Megan out the driveway.

"Is it back to the usual grind tomorrow?" he asked her.

"Yep. We open at six for breakfast like always. But we'll be closed for New Year's Day, so that's a plus."

"My business slows after Christmas," Paul said. "The freight companies are busy keeping stores stocked for Christmas shopping, then it comes to a screeching halt until the middle of January when stores start putting winter stuff on clearance to make room for spring designs. The slowdown will give me a chance to hire and train an assistant."

Candy said, "I'm making Tracy the manager at the café. I'll start teaching her the process for ordering. I will still pay the bills, but she'll be doing the rest. She already helps with the scheduling."

Paul pulled into Candy's driveway. He helped her out of the car, carried the dishes in for her and placed them on the kitchen cabinet.

Candy said, "Would you like to stay? I'm sure there's a movie on the television."

Paul realized he didn't look forward to the solitude of an empty apartment like he used to. "Sure. You pick."

Candy grinned, "You're in luck. I like action movies. Save me from chick flicks."

Paul smiled, "Don't let that information out. Guys will be lining up to date you if they don't have to sit through a mushy tearjerker of a movie."

Candy was looking through the guide and said, "Here's a good World War II movie. How about that?"

"Perfect."

Paul and Candy settled on the couch to watch the movie. Halfway through, Candy paused it to make popcorn and pour sodas.

When the movie was over Paul said, "I'd better go. Thanks for going with me to the Stone's and for the movie. It's been a good day."

"Yes, it has," Candy replied. "Thank you for the invitation."

When Candy closed the door behind Paul, she felt a sense of contentment about her day. As Paul walked to his car, he, too, was feeling good about his Christmas Day. He drove away smiling.

Chapter 18

I n early January, Paul and Candy met at Rich's office where they finished the paperwork for a business license and a limited liability corporation. Cotton Garner enterprises was official.

As they walked to their cars outside of Rich's office Candy said, "I'm excited, but I have some huge butterflies in the pit of my stomach."

Paul smiled, "That's normal. That's how I felt when I left teaching, took a truck driving course and then started the logistics business."

Candy looked surprised, "You taught? I didn't know that. What did you teach?"

"I tried to teach math. I liked the kids, and I think the kids liked me. I even liked preparing lessons. But I hated having to be in one place all day long. I felt claustrophobic. I was always good with logics and puzzles, and I sort of stumbled on the idea of connecting vendors with freight haulers. Some companies have their own logistics people, but most prefer to contract with me instead of hiring a person and paying out all the benefits. It works."

"Interesting," Candy said. "I've never thought of doing anything except cooking or running the café. I like it."

"It shows," Paul said. "Are you going back to the café?"

"Yes. It's almost time for the lunch rush, and I have one waitress out sick with the flu."

Paul said, "I'm going to the office. Chip is doing the finishing touches on it. I want to measure then go buy furniture. How do you feel about just painting the walls and refinishing the hardwood floors on the second level for now? We can make changes when we know what is going in there."

"Sure. That sounds reasonable. Maybe Tonya can photograph it and let out the word that an interesting historical space is for rent."

"Good idea. I'll tell Chip." He waved to Candy and called, "I will probably be down for dinner. I have a busy day, and I know I won't have time to cook."

Candy smiled, "OK. See you then."

Tonya DeBoe returned in early February. She photographed Paul's office, the second floor, and the progress on the first floor.

"You have vision, Paul," she said.

"Not me," he replied. "Candy. I needed an office. The rest of this is all her planning. She was the one who gave me the idea to even buy this building. Chip and Jacob completely overhauled the electric and plumbing. They were even able to blow some insulation behind some of the walls."

"Can I walk over and talk with Candy?" Tonya asked.

"Sure, let's go." Paul locked the building and walked with Tonya across the street to the café.

Candy spotted Tonya coming through the door.

"Tonya, welcome back. It's good to see you again."

Tonya smiled, "It's nice to see you too, Candy. I love what you're doing with the building across the street."

Candy said, "Me, too. I have loved that old place since I was a kid. I hated to see it empty and deteriorating. Now, I can't wait to see how the bakery works out. I hope it goes well."

Tonya said, "I'm sure it will, especially if you sell your meals-to-go from there. Everyone always wants dessert. I can't believe all the new housing developments that have gone up near the interstate since I was here last year. That has to be good for your business."

Candy said, "Some. The Saturday crowd has grown. Most of those people work in Winston Salem and are rarely in Whitlow during the weekdays. A retired couple moved here and opened a bookstore down the street. That brings in a few shoppers during the day who come in for lunch, so that helps. The couple said they saw Whitlow featured in your magazine, so we can thank you for their coming."

Paul saw some acquaintances and stepped over to speak with them.

Tonya leaned toward Candy and said, "I just have to ask, how did you talk Paul into going into business with you? You can't fail with him. Chase, my husband, says he is a money-making machine."

Candy said, "I didn't. He asked me."

Tonya looked at Candy intently, "Really? You must be special, then. I've never known Paul to partner with any-one before."

Candy smiled, "It's working out well. I hope it continues that way." Tonya ordered a large coffee to go and left.

Chapter 19

C andy circled April 1 on her calendar. That was the opening day for the bakery. She had just a little over a month to order supplies and get them delivered. She would start baking the cookies a week before and freeze them. They would be decorated on March 31. Everything else would be baked a day or two before the opening and kept refrigerated or baked the morning of opening day.

After weeks of hard work and late night prepping, April 1 finally arrived. Candy still couldn't believe that her dream of owning her own bakery was actually coming true. She put an apron over her clothes, ready for business. Ellen, a waitress from the café, had been scheduled to wait on customers. Paul stood in the dining area with Tonya who had been taking pictures.

Candy transferred the decorated cakes from the kitchen to the display case.

She took a deep breath, looked at Paul and said, "Unlock the door."

The first people to come in were from the newspaper to take pictures and get the information for the next edition. The couple who owned the bookstore came in to buy muffins and coffee. Several women who power walked three mornings a week stopped in to see the new business. Each one left with a bottle of water and a bag of cookies decorated like Easter eggs.

All morning long, a steady stream of curious people came in. Some just wanted to see the inside of the building but ended up leaving with a baked good and a drink.

Tonya got a few more pictures then left. Candy gave Ellen a lunch break and sat down behind the counter.

"Are you alright?" Paul asked. He had been present ever since he unlocked the door.

"Yes. I think my nervousness is starting to go away, but I'm tired from the stress of the unknown."

Paul smiled, "I understand."

The phone rang. Candy answered questions and gave out prices. When it rang again, Candy took orders for evening meals in her new to-go business.

The afternoon sped by. At six, Paul turned the open sign to closed and locked the door. He turned around to face Candy. He grinned and swept her up in a tight hug.

"You did it! You made your bakery dream come true."

Paul swung her around. He held her as she slowly slid down his body until her feet touched the floor. Paul suddenly saw her for the truly beautiful woman she was. He bent down and kissed her lightly then looked at her to gauge her reaction.

The contact with Paul gave Candy goose bumps, and

the kiss made her catch her breath. As she looked into Paul's eyes, Candy wasted no time. She put her arms around Paul's neck and pulled him in for another kiss. Paul tightened his arms around her and deepened the kiss. Soon they were both breathless, their heart rates rising.

Paul released her and smiled. "That was an unexpected ending to a great day."

He traced her chin with his index finger and said, "I had a hard time ending that kiss. You are a very desirable woman, Candy Cotton."

Candy smiled. No man had ever called her desirable before.

She looked into his eyes and said, "I had a hard time ending it as well. I liked kissing you."

Paul took her face in his hands and kissed her again.

"Come on, I'll help you clean up." The two put the leftover cakes, muffins, cupcakes and cookies in the refrigerator. They would be reduced in price the next day.

When they were finished, Paul took Candy's hand and led her across the street to the café. Tracy was getting ready to close when they walked through the door.

"How did the first day go?" Tracy asked Candy.

"I was pleased. I hope the traffic picks up a little more, but it's only the first day. It will come and go just like the business here. How was your first day as official manager?"

"Good. It felt like any other day. We have a little food

left over from the to-go business. I'm going to put that on special tomorrow for lunch."

"Good idea," Candy said. "Go on home. I'll finish up here. I'm too wired to go home. This will help me settle down and calm the nerves."

Tracy smiled, "You don't have to tell me twice. Thanks." Candy smiled as she watched Tracy leave.

Paul had been watching.

"That was nice of you, Candy. It's no wonder your employees are loyal, and you have so little turnover."

Candy smiled, "I just treat them the way I want to be treated."

Paul sat at the counter while Candy finished cleaning the table tops and took the dishes out of the washer. She took a stack of napkins and a tray of forks and gave them to Paul.

She said, "Here, make yourself useful. You can wrap these forks for in the morning."

Paul smiled and wrapped forks while Candy secured the kitchen for the night. When she was finished, she took the silverware from Paul, kissed him quickly and said, "Thanks."

"I'm hooked," he said. "I will wrap forks all night if I get kisses."

Candy grinned, "The price may go up. You may have to wrap forks and knives for more kisses."

Paul laughed and pulled her to him. "Miss Cotton, you are amazing, and you make me laugh." He leaned in for another long, lingering kiss.

Candy broke the kiss and said, "Mr. Garner, I have an early morning. I need to go home."

Paul sighed and said, "I'll walk you to your car. I don't want a repeat of Halloween ever again."

"Thanks," she said. "Neither do I."

Within a month, word had spread about the bakery. Candy was receiving orders for decorated cakes, and the coffee shop at the interstate bought all the muffins Candy could deliver. After doing the accounting, Candy found the first month had been profitable. It was only a slight profit, but that was better than ending the month with a loss.

If business continued to grow, she was going to need more help than a waitress making coffee and running the cash register. She made a note to call the community college in the morning to see if there were any students about to graduate who were interested in baking.

Paul put his head into the doorway of her office and said, "It's quitting time. Want to go for pizza?"

Candy smiled. "Sure. I'll lock up here then go across to

make sure the café is ready for closing."

"When are you going to start parking over here and trusting Tracy to make sure the café opens and closes without incident?"

Candy blushed, "I know. I'm having a hard time letting go. That's my baby over there. She's doing a great job, and you're right. I do need to cut the apron strings."

She sighed, "I'll start parking over here. Then I won't have an excuse to go there every night."

Paul smiled, "That's my girl. Now you're thinking like a CEO."

Candy rolled her eyes. "I don't feel like a CEO. I feel like a manager trying to stay above water."

"We all do, Candy. That never changes."

The two walked across the street, closed the café, and Paul drove them to the pizza restaurant at the interstate.

Chapter 20

T he bakery kept a steady stream of customers. The most profitable products were the muffins and decorated cakes. Candy's reputation as a cake decorator spread, and she was starting to get requests for wedding cakes.

In the office upstairs, Paul's newly hired assistant worked to monitor the routes and schedules for Garner Logistics. This left Paul with more time to monitor Blue Ridge Properties and Cotton Garner Enterprises. He was reading a report from the property company when he got a call from the manager.

"Good morning, Ted. What can I do for you?" Paul asked.

"There's a property for sale up here that I thought you might be interested in. It's an old house. Since you've been in two magazine articles for historical restorations, I thought you might be interested."

Paul said, "Send pictures and information. The historical thing just randomly happened. It's not a life calling or anything. If I buy something like that, I'd rather buy it here. My brother and his friend are the ones who work the magic on those places."

"OK. I'll email you the information. Just let me know what you decide. Since you're in North Carolina most of the time, do you still want me to search out properties here?"

"Sure, Ted. You can continue to look for them there. If you have time, check out the areas here around Whitlow and Winston Salem. I can always drive by the places to make sure they aren't being abused."

"Sure thing," Ted said. "I'll watch the listings in your area. Talk with you later."

Paul said, "Awesome. Tell Cathy hello for me."

"Will do." Ted ended the call.

Candy was working on the bills for the bakery. She had an idea she wanted to try, so she took the elevator to Paul's office. When she walked onto the third floor, his new assistant was at a desk in the lobby.

"Good morning, Brian. Is Paul in?" she asked.

"Yes, but he's on the phone with Blue Ridge Properties right now," he answered.

Candy looked confused. "Is there a problem with the building across the street?"

"Not that I know of," Brian answered. "He usually gets one or two calls a week from the manager."

Now Candy was really confused.

"Why would that property company be calling Paul?"

she asked.

Brian shrugged. "I don't know, I just assumed it was because he owned the company."

Candy felt her face flush with shock. Her heart sank and her stomach did a somersault. She felt hurt and angry.

"He does?" she asked.

Brian answered, "Yes. I thought you knew since you' re his partner with the bakery."

"No, I didn't know that," Candy said, trying to keep her voice calm in spite of the anger that was growing in her chest.

"Didn't know what?" Paul asked as he came up behind her. He smiled at her and said, "You look nice this morning."

Candy glared at him.

"Whoa," Paul said. "What happened? You look angry."

"Do you or do you not own the building you live in?"

Paul looked confused, "Blue Ridge Properties owns the building."

"Do you own Blue Ridge Properties?"

"Yes," Paul said, "but my name is not on the deed for that building. Blue Ridge Properties owns it."

"But you bought it in the property company's name," Candy said.

"I didn't buy it, Candy. The property company did," Paul said. "What's the problem? Did something go wrong in the café? I can call the manager to have it taken care of."

"No. Nothing is wrong except that you lied about paying rent to a landlord," Candy said.

"I do pay rent," Paul said. "I pay rent to Blue Ridge Properties just like you do, because they own the property."

Candy let out a groan in frustration. "OK, Blue Ridge Properties owns the building, but you own Blue Ridge Properties. Am I right?"

Paul said, "It's a corporation, but yes, the company is mine. Is that a problem?"

Candy lost her temper, "I cannot believe that you bought that building, that I have been paying you rent for a year, and that you never told me the truth."

"Candy, I pay rent, too. I didn't think it was a big deal. Are you not happy with the building or the repairs the company made in your kitchen?"

"OOHH, you are so frustrating," Candy yelled. "That is not the point! The point is that you did not tell me the truth."

"Candy, please calm down so we can discuss this rationally," Paul said, trying to stay calm.

"No. I will not calm down. I am angry. You were not truthful with me!"

"I was," Paul said. "You've known all along that Blue Ridge Properties bought the building. That has never been a lie."

Candy opened her mouth to speak but closed it again. She took a deep breath and said, "I'm leaving. I have a business to run. I don't want to talk to you anymore."

"Candy, I think we need to resolve this."

"No. Don't talk to me. Leave me alone." Candy stomped out of the office and took the stairs back to the bakery.

Paul looked around at Brian who was trying to make himself as small as possible.

Paul asked, "How did Candy find out I own Blue Ridge Properties?"

Brian said, "You were on the phone with them when she came in. I mentioned that. She got all upset thinking something was wrong with your building. I reassured her you get several calls a week from them. When she asked why, I shrugged and said probably because you own the company. You guys are partners, I had no idea she didn't know about that."

Paul looked at Brian. The young man had just broken a cardinal policy he had put in place for employees.

"Brian, Candy has no part in that company. I don't cross lines with the companies. Each company stays in its own compartment. She had no need to know I own Blue Ridge Properties. You had no business telling her that I did."

Brian said, "Sorry, Paul. I just assumed she knew."

Paul said, "I seem to recall telling you this very thing when I was training you, do you remember that?"

"I think so," Brian said.

Paul went to his office then brought back a sheet of paper with Brian's signature.

"This is an agreement that you signed stating that you would not talk to anyone about anything having to do with my companies."

"But I thought she knew," Brian said.

Paul said, "The key words here are anyone and anything. In other words, you don't talk about my companies at all."

Paul sighed, "Your ninety-day probation is now over. You will not be hired permanently. You can clear out your desk and leave. And this agreement also says that if you talk about my businesses after you leave employment here, I can sue you for breach of contract. Care to read it?"

"No, sir." Brian replied.

Paul went back into his office. He was furious. How was he going to fix this with Candy? He really liked her and thought their relationship was going in the right direction.

Paul went back to the lobby. "I need your key, Brian."

Brian took the office key off his keyring and handed it to Paul.

"Thank you."

Paul turned around and went back to his office. He wondered if he had been too hard on Brian, but he decided he hadn't. He needed people he could trust working for him. If Brian had been so quick to make a mistake with this, who knew what kind of mistake he would make with the schedules.

Paul listened as Brian left the office. He let out a long breath and contemplated what to do next. Paul leaned back in his desk chair and sighed. What a mess, he thought. If he had known Candy would react like this without remembering how much she had profited from his actions, he would have never bought the building, either building. He absolutely did not understand her reaction or thought process. Evidently, her feelings toward him were not as solid as he had hoped.

Pulling out his cell phone, Paul punched in Chip's phone number. "Hey, what's up?" Chip asked.

"Candy found out I own her café's building," Paul said flatly.

Chip paused for a moment, reading a lot in Paul's tone of voice. "I gather she didn't take it well."

"No, she did not. To say she was angry would be an understatement. She was more like irrationally hostile."

"Ouch," Chip said. "What are you going to do?"

"She's downstairs in the bakery. She doesn't want to talk to me and straighten this out. I will give her a day to calm down. If she's still angry, I'll have to come up with some type of plan. If I had known it would come to this, I would've gone back to Philly, never purchased either building and just stayed in the motel when I came to visit. But then you and Jacob would not be in the position you are in now. That, at least, is a positive outcome of all this."

"I hate to feel like I've gained from your misfortune, though," Chip said.

"Don't feel that way. I'm proud of what you and Jacob have started. I'm glad I had a hand in it," Paul replied. "I'm going back to my apartment to work from there and try to decide what I'm going to do if Candy persists in being angry. She's back to her old habit of hating me, and I'm tired of that. It's not worth the effort."

"I get that," Chip said. "I was getting tired of it, too. I called her out on it more than once, but nothing worked until the incident on Halloween."

Paul sighed, "Yeah. I'm beginning to realize everything is all about her. She's all take and no give, well except for the occasional large tea in the mornings."

"Man," Chip continued, "You would think that with all you've done for her with the bakery that she would over-look this, laugh about it and appreciate your efforts. This is unbelievable."

"Well, I have a lot to think about. I'm going to work from home. I don't want to risk running into her here in the building. Neither one of us would enjoy that. I'll talk to you later," Paul said.

"Sure." Chip ended the call.

Paul left his office building from the back where his car was parked. He drove the two blocks to the back of the café and went inside. Knowing Candy was across the street, Paul went to the lunch counter and ordered his usual tea.

Tracy handed him the tea and said, "What are you doing over here? I thought you had an office."

Paul smiled, "I had a problem with the assistant. I let him go. I decided to work from home again until I figure out what I want to do."

Tracy said, "Well, if you want to hire someone else, I have a prospect for you. Mike and I have a friend who has always worked in the information technology arena. He's very sharp with computers. He just lost his job because the company he worked for was mismanaged and went bankrupt. He's in his thirties and more mature than that baby you hired."

Paul chuckled, "Baby is right. He couldn't even grasp the depth of his mistake and the ramifications a similar breech in policy could have on my business."

Paul handed Tracy the money for the tea and said, "Thanks. My workload has suddenly increased again, and I need to get on it. See you later."

"Sure," Tracy said as she watched Paul leave.

She could tell he was upset. That assistant must have messed up miserably.

Chip called Megan.

"Hey, honey, what's going on?" Megan asked.

He said, "I know we were going to meet at the café for lunch, but would you mind if I got a couple sandwiches and drinks from the food truck parked at the grocery store?"

"That's fine with me, but I sense there is a reason for this."

Chip answered, "There is. I'll tell you everything when I get there. See you in a few minutes."

Chip ended the call, got out of his truck and walked to the mobile sandwich shop. He ordered two club sandwiches, chips and drinks then drove to Megan's office. When he walked in, Megan smiled, took the food, and pointed to a chair at her conference table.

"Sit. I want to know what has happened. Obviously, Candy is involved if you don't want to eat at the café."

Chip told Megan about Candy's discovery that Paul owned her building and the reaction she had. He told her how upset Paul was and that he's not sure Paul is going to stay in town.

"Oh, no!" Megan exclaimed. "He can't leave now; the baby is due any day. Surely, he wants to meet his nephew."

"I don't think he has even thought about that. I'll use it as leverage to keep him in town for a while," Chip replied.

Megan sighed, "I knew Candy was volatile and occasionally irrational, but this just takes the cake, no pun intended. After all that Paul has done for her, she can't take this in stride and just say thank you? I'm disappointed in her. I knew she could be self centered, but this is beyond that definition. She's acting like a teenager, not a grown woman with a business."

Chip agreed. They ate in silence for a moment.

"You know, Paul said the one thing that made all this trouble worth it was the business Jacob and I have started and that it's successful. That's just like Paul. He's always looked for what he could do for someone else, not what someone else could do for him."

When they had finished eating, Chip kissed Megan on the cheek and said, "I need to get back to work. I'll convince Paul to stay until after the baby comes. He just forgot about that because of all that's happened."

Megan smiled and said, "Thanks."

Chapter 21

The next morning, Paul called Chip. "Hey, Paul," Chip said. "I was about to call you. Are you still thinking about leaving town?"

"Yes. That's why I'm calling," Paul replied.

Chip said, "Well, forget that plan. Megan had the baby early this morning. You need to come and meet your nephew."

Paul laughed, "Wow, congratulations! Are you at the local hospital?"

"Yes. Room 309. The nursery is on the same floor."

"Can I come now?" Paul asked.

"Of course. That's why I was about to call you. They're both ready to receive visitors."

"I'm on my way," Paul said.

Paul walked to the florist next door and bought a large bouquet of yellow roses and tulips. He also bought a vase in which to place them when he got to Megan's room. A nephew. The next generation of Garners. Suddenly, he couldn't wait to get to the hospital to see Chip and meet the little guy.

Paul juggled the flowers and vase as he got off the elevator on the third floor of the hospital. The nursery was right in front of him. He slowly walked along the large windows looking for baby boy Garner. There he was, right in the front row where he could be seen. Paul looked at him and felt a sense of uncle pride growing.

The baby held Paul's attention so intensely that he had not noticed the woman standing beside him.

He looked at her and asked, "Is there a new baby in your family, too?"

She turned to him, smiled, pointed to baby boy Garner and said, "That handsome fellow is my new cousin. His mother and I grew up together, and we are almost as close as sisters."

Paul looked at her with surprise. He said, "That hand-some fellow is my new nephew."

The woman smiled, extended her hand and said, "I'm Samantha Albright, Megan's cousin."

Paul shook her hand and said, "I'm Paul Garner, Chip's brother." Paul looked at her in confusion, "I don't remember seeing you at the wedding."

Samantha's face fell, "You didn't. I was out of the country and there were problems with my flights when I was trying to return. I missed the wedding. I was so upset."

Paul said, "It was a nice wedding, but a typical short, sweet ceremony and reception. You know, the usual."

Samantha grinned, "A typical man's opinion, which I can't fault you for. We females are much more sentimental about such things."

Paul said, "I guess there's a balance in everything. Have you seen Megan?"

"No," she replied. "I've been staring at the baby. I take it you haven't been in either."

"No. I was just about to go to their room. Want to go with me?"

"Sure."

Samantha turned and the two looked for room 309. Chip came out of the room just as they found it.

"Paul! Samantha! Come in. Have you seen him? I was just going to get him."

"Yes." Samantha replied. "He's beautiful."

Chip held the door open and said, "Go on in. I'll bring the baby back."

Samantha and Paul entered the room.

"Sam!" Megan exclaimed. "I'm so happy to see you!"

She looked at Paul, "I'm happy to see you too, Paul, but it's been much longer since Samantha and I have seen each other."

"It's OK, Megan. I'm not hurt.... too much," he said grinning.

"Oh, you," Megan said. She patted the bed beside her. "Sit, Sam, I want to know everything you've been doing."

Before Sam could say anything, Chip came into the room pushing the baby's bassinette.

He picked up the child and said, "Paul, Sam, meet Jonathan Banks Garner," and he handed the baby to Paul.

Paul gently took Jonathan, bounced him slightly and said, "Dad would be proud, Chip. Another Jonathan Garner to take on the world."

After a few minutes he looked at Samantha, "Want to hold him?"

Samantha grinned and held out her hands, "Of course I do." Samantha took Jonathan and held him close. "I like that you put Banks in his name. Grandpa would be happy about that."

Megan looked at Paul and said, "Banks Albright was our grandfather. He took us for rides in the back of his truck, took us fishing, sneaked us candy when our moms said no, and doted on us. He even bought each of us our first car. I still miss him."

"Me too," Samantha said, smiling at the memories.

Paul studied Samantha while she talked with Megan. She was attractive with a girl next door look about her. She wore little make up, and her eyes were a nondescript hazel. Her light brown hair was cut short and curled around her earlobe toward her cheek. Samantha was not the sort of woman who would grab your attention in a crowd, but once you met her, you would not forget her.

Paul decided that what drew your attention was her personality. She was unassuming, friendly, and had a surprising sense of humor. Her smile was wide and sincere. Then he realized that she put everyone around her at ease. She dissolved tension instead of creating it. He was fascinated.

Chip pulled Paul to the side while Samantha talked with Megan.

"I'm glad you're still in town. Megan was distraught when she thought you might not be here for the birth. She loves you like a brother and values your presence in her life."

"I feel the same about her," Paul said. "You married a jewel. And now look, you're a dad. It must feel amazing."

"It does," Chip said, "and a little scary."

"I'm sure," Paul replied. The dietary staff came into the room with two lunch trays.

Paul said, "This is my cue to leave. I'll be back. Well, maybe, when do you go home?"

"Tomorrow," Chip said. "There were no complications with either Megan or Jonathan."

"I'm glad to hear that. Call me when you get home," Paul said. "I'll drop by for a visit."

"Sounds like a plan," Chip said.

Samantha said goodbye to Chip and Megan and followed Paul out the door.

"He's a beautiful baby," Samantha said.

"Yes, he is." Paul looked at Samantha, "Would you like to get some lunch? After all, we have a new baby relative in common."

Samantha smiled, "I'd like that. Where do you suggest? Megan always talks about a café downtown."

Paul thought for a moment. It was the best option. Candy wouldn't be working there, so it should be safe.

Paul said, "We can go there. It has great food."

"I'll follow you in my car," she said.

Paul drove to the edge of the parking lot and waited for Samantha. When she pulled up behind him, he turned onto the connector street and drove to Main Street. He found two parking slots beside each other and pulled into one. Samantha pulled into the other one.

They walked along two store fronts to the café. Paul opened the door for Samantha, the two went inside, and he led her to a booth. A waitress came to take their drink orders and left them to look at the menu.

"Do you eat here often?" Samantha asked.

"Yes. It's convenient. I live in the apartment upstairs," he answered.

Samantha grinned, "You live in the place that has that great balcony overlooking the street?"

"Yep. I own the building, and I renovated the whole second floor for an apartment after Chip moved here. He's all the family I have left. I believe in keeping family close."

Samantha smiled, "I believe that, too. That's why I was so sad I missed the wedding."

Samantha looked around her and said, "Wait, this is the place in the American Design magazine. You live in the apartment Chip designed and built."

"Yes. Well, I helped in the sense that I had to approve the final plans."

Paul laughed, "He presented three plans from low cost

to expensive. I made his head spin when I took pieces of all three and combined them. But I love the results. Would you like to see it? I'll take you up there after we eat."

"I would love to see it. Didn't he do the building across the street? Could we go see that too?" she asked.

Paul hesitated for a moment but said, "Sure. I'll show you the top two floors. The bakery speaks for itself. I highly recommend getting the almond sugar cookies. Candy, who is part owner, is a food genius. Everything she makes is delicious. She owns this café. All the dishes are her recipes."

Tracy came over to the table to take their order. "Hey Paul, what are ya'll having?"

Paul said, "Tracy, this is Samantha Albright. She's Megan's cousin and came into town because Megan had her baby last night."

Tracy smiled, "That's wonderful. I heard she was having a boy."

"She did," Paul said. Samantha and Paul gave Tracy their orders and resumed their conversation.

Paul said, "So, you were out of the country for the wedding. Was it business or pleasure?"

"Business," Samantha said, "and call me Sam. Everyone else does."

"Alright, Sam, what do you do, if I may ask?"

"I'm in international sales. I work for the Regal Food Company in Richmond. I handle the sales side of their export division," she explained.

"That sounds interesting. How did you get into that?" he asked.

"I have a business degree, and I speak several languages, which always helps," Sam explained. "What do you do?"

"I own Garner Logistics which pairs merchants and manufacturers with freight haulers. I also own a properties company, and I now co-own the bakery," he said.

"Quite a diverse portfolio," she said. "How did you get into all that?"

"Quite by accident. I started teaching but hated the restrictions of being in a classroom all day. Took a truck driving course, liked the business side and started the logistics firm. I stumbled on some amazing property deals and started the property company. Then I decided to bankroll Candy Cotton's expansion into the bakery and catering business because she's talented and has a good business sense. If I see something I think will turn a profit, I'm always willing to consider it."

"Fascinating," Sam said, "And you're right. This food is delicious."

Paul grinned, "Wait until you taste the cookies."

Chapter 22

C andy happened to look out the bakery window to see Paul walking into the café with a woman she had not seen before. Even though she was still furious with Paul, a feeling of jealousy shot through her chest. She began tapping her toes on the floor and felt her cheeks flush with anger. They have one little spat, and he takes another woman to lunch. That's nerve.

Candy took off her apron and said to the cashier, "Ellen, I need to go to the café. I'll be right back."

Before Ellen could respond, Candy stormed out the door and across the street. Taking a deep breath, she opened the door and walked to the back of the cafe looking for Tracy. She found the woman in the office.

Candy walked into the office, closed the door, and asked, "Who's that with Paul?"

Tracy looked up and said, "Hello, Candy. I wondered if you had seen him come in. To answer your question, that is Samantha Albright, Megan's cousin. Megan had the baby last night, and Samantha came into town to see her. Chip called Paul and the two just happened to be at the hospital at the same time. It's lunch, so I guess they decided to eat together. Any more questions?"

"No. That's it. Megan had her baby?"

"Yes. A boy as expected," Tracy answered.

"Thanks for telling me. I need to go see them."

Candy opened the door and started to walk back through the café. She took a deep breath and stopped at Paul's table.

"Hello, Paul," she said, "I heard Megan had her baby. Congratulations on a new nephew."

"Thanks, Candy," he replied. "Candy this is Samantha Albright, Megan's cousin. Sam, this is Candy Cotton, she owns the café."

Sam said, "It's nice to meet you, Candy. The food here is delicious. Paul has highly recommended I try your sugar cookies in the bakery. I'll get some before I leave."

Paul watched Sam work her soothing magic on Candy.

Candy relaxed and smiled.

"Thank you, Samantha. I'm glad you like your lunch. Are you going to be in town long?"

"I'm staying the night at the motel then going back to Richmond tomorrow."

Candy smiled, "I hope you enjoy your time with Megan. She's a good friend of mine, and I'm glad she has family to share her joy. I need to get back to work. Nice to meet you."

"It was nice to meet you, too," Sam said, and she watched Candy walk out the door.

Sam looked at Paul, "I gather that is your partner in the bakery."

"That's the one," Paul said sarcastically.

Sam raised her eyebrow. "Trouble in paradise?"

Paul took a deep breath, "You might say that. We have had a big difference of opinion. I'm thinking of becoming the most silent partner ever in a business deal and leave town. It's that bad. She can email me the financials. The partnership will be profitable, no doubt. We just have different personalities and points of view."

"Bummer," Sam said. "I would think owning a bakery would be fun."

"It could have been. She's the boss there. I wouldn't tell her how to run that bakery for anything. I would mess it up. But I own the building. The second floor is vacant, and my offices are on the third floor. I'm going to rent both out, so, I will recoup my investment with no problem."

Paul took the check and stood. "Let me take care of this, and I'll show you the apartment upstairs." Paul paid the bill and said bye to Tracy as he and Sam walked out the back of the café.

He turned to Sam and said, "I'll go first and unlock the door." Sam followed him.

When they entered, she said, "The pictures did not do this justice. This is beautiful." Sam walked around inspecting the kitchen, living area and the gas log fireplace.

When she got to the balcony, Sam said, "I would stay out there all the time."

Paul agreed. "I've really enjoyed that aspect of the place. Let me show you the rest of the apartment, especially the master suite."

He showed her the spare bedroom and hall bathroom then opened the door to the master bedroom.

Sam looked at the sitting and sleeping areas before walking into the bathroom with its huge closets.

"Wow. No wonder you like this place. Will you be able to rent it out for the money you have in it?"

"Probably not, but I've lived here for over a year, and I guess you could say it's been broken in. But I may keep it. I plan to visit Jonathan, Chip and Megan as much as I can."

"I would keep it for myself," Sam said.

Paul shrugged, "I probably will. I won't make a hasty decision. Do you want to see the other building?"

"Yes. I want to see if it outshines the pictures in the magazine, too. Seeing these places gives me a glimpse at what Chip can do with an old building. He's amazing."

Paul smiled, "Yes, he is. Come on, we'll go across the street."

Paul led Sam back through the café and across the street. They entered the building and took the elevator to the third floor.

"This floor holds the logistic company's offices," he said.

Sam looked at the layout and the décor. "Nice," she said.

Paul led her back to his office. "I like my comfort."

Sam chuckled, "I should say so. You could just live in here!"

Paul took her down the stairs and showed her the second floor with its new paint and gleaming hardwood floors. When they got back to the first floor, he opened the door to the bakery. Sam walked in and looked around.

"I love the ceiling and the original wood. Was the fireplace always here?" she asked.

"Chip found it behind a wall. We opened the ventilation and put in gas logs."

Candy stood behind the counter and watched Sam inspect her bakery. She wanted to feel proud, but instead she was annoyed. She wanted them to leave.

"Would you like to try anything?" she asked.

Sam smiled, "I would like six sugar cookies and six oatmeal cookies," she said. Candy filled the order, and Sam paid the bill.

"Thank you, Candy. I look forward to tasting these."

"You're welcome, Sam. I hope you come again the next time you're in town," Candy replied.

Sam smiled then turned to Paul, "Shall we go?"

"Sure." He turned to Candy, "See you later, Candy."

Paul held the door and walked out with Sam. Candy rolled her eyes with annoyance, glad they were gone.

When they were out of the building, Sam asked, "Is Candy always this prickly?"

"She was at first, then things got better. Now she's back

to her former self, only worse," Paul said with a hint of sadness in his voice.

"What are you going to do about the partnership, if I may ask."

"I'm going to give her a plan to buy me out. Then she will be just a renter. The business is so new it will take her a few years, but that's OK. I won't be here."

Sam said, "I'm sorry, but I just met her, and already I can't blame you for wanting out. Good luck."

"Thanks. What are your plans for the afternoon?"

"I'm going to see if the motel has any empty rooms. I would like to stay over and visit Megan tomorrow before going back to Richmond."

"You don't have a room?" Paul asked.

"Not yet," she answered.

"You're welcome to stay in my guest room. No one has ever used it. You can use my Wi-Fi if you need to work,"

Sam thought for a moment then said, "Alright. Thanks, I'll take you up on that. It'll be a lot nicer than the monotonous hotel rooms I usually stay in."

"Good. Get your car and follow me. We'll park in the back."

Paul backed into the street, pulled up and waited for Sam to get behind him. He circled the block then pulled into his parking place behind the building. He motioned Sam to park beside him.

Sam carried her computer, and Paul carried her overnight bag up the stairs. He placed it on the bed in the spare room.

He said, "The hall bathroom is yours. Make yourself at home. Come with me. I want to show you something."

Sam followed Paul into the den. He went to the wall that had a picture in a large frame on the wall and a chair in front. He moved the chair, flipped two latches and lowered the picture.

Sam exclaimed, "It's a murphy desk! How ingenious."

Paul smiled, "I had this done in case I really did have a visitor who needed to work from here. I work from the desk in my bedroom."

He handed her a piece of paper, "This is the Wi-Fi password." Paul grinned and said, "You must promise to guard it with your life."

Sam laughed, "On my honor, I will protect and defend this password."

Paul opened the refrigerator and said, "There are sodas, bottled water, a few beers, and some iced tea from the café. Help yourself. Mi casa es su casa."

Sam smiled, "Gracias."

Placing her computer on the desk she said, "I'm going to change and do about two hours of work. Will that be alright?"

"Perfect," Paul said. "I'll do the same."

Two hours later, Paul emerged from his room in jeans and a t-shirt. He went into the kitchen, took two steaks from the refrigerator and placed them in a marinade. He wrapped two potatoes in foil, put them in the oven and set the timer for an hour.

Sam closed her computer. "That looks like you were expecting company."

"No. They came from the grocer this way. I would have frozen the extra steak and eventually eaten the extra potatoes before they rotted," Paul explained. He took two bottles of water from the refrigerator.

Handing one to Sam, he said, "Want to take a walk? Sometimes I feel like I need one after I've been in front of a computer for several hours."

"I would love that. You can show me the town."

Paul and Sam walked on the sidewalk down Main Street to the park. They crossed the street, and Sam looked in every store front as they walked back toward the apartment. When they returned, Paul took two beers out of the refrigerator, and they sat on the balcony.

"Paul, this is lovely. I see why you like it here. I had forgotten how quaint and quiet Whitlow is. It's been a long time since I was here," Sam said. "What have you seen from your balcony?"

"Halloween was the best. The kids dressed up and went trick-or-treating from store to store and through the park. Megan, Chip and some friends came over to watch the Christmas parade, which was fun. Other than that, I just sit out here and watch the seasons change."

"May I make a reservation for Halloween?" Sam asked. "I would love to see that. I can just see Megan and Chip dressing up Jonathan in a baby costume."

Paul laughed, "I wouldn't doubt it, and yes, you have a standing invitation to the balcony whenever you want."

Paul heard the alarm on the oven. "Hungry?" he asked. "Yes."

"Alright, you can help with dinner." Paul took vegetables out of the crisper and two bowls from the cabinet. "You make the salads."

While Sam cut and diced vegetables, Paul took the steaks and placed them on the grill at the back of his stove top.

Sam looked over and said, "You have one of those downward ventilated grills. I am determined to have one in any house I own."

"They're handy," Paul said. "I knew I would have nowhere to grill outside, so I had this installed. It was one of those changes that made Chip's head spin," he said laughing.

Paul plated the steaks and potatoes and took them to the table. Sam placed the salads and silverware by them while Paul opened a bottle of wine that had been chilling. He took the bottle to the table where he filled two glasses.

They sat down for dinner. Sam raised her glass and said, "To baby Jonathan Banks Garner."

Paul met her toast with the clink of glasses.

Then Paul said, "To new friendships formed around a new baby."

Sam smiled and the glasses clinked again. Sam bit into

her steak.

"This is delicious. What did you marinate it in?"

"I have a few ingredients I like with steak. I'll write them down for you. It's just a little of this and that."

"I want the recipe for this and that," Sam said.

The two talked over dinner and into the night.

Finally, Sam yawned and said, "My word, it's after midnight! No wonder I'm getting sleepy. I left Richmond early this morning." She stood, "I'm going to have to go to bed or I won't be able to stay awake tomorrow."

Paul stood, "I'll turn out the lights. Make yourself at home. Sleep in if you want; I'll be here. I have a cheese Danish from Candy's in the refrigerator for breakfast."

Sam smiled, "You think of everything, Mr. Host of the Year."

The next morning, Paul woke before Sam. He started the coffee and put the Danish pastry on the cabinet to begin warming to room temperature. A few minutes, later he heard Sam coming down the hall.

"I smell coffee," Sam said, "wonderful, wonderful coffee."

Paul grinned and filled her a cup. "Sugar or cream?" he asked.

"Cream, please." Paul handed her a carton of heavy cream.

"Mmmm, that's good," she said. "Now I can wake up."

When Paul handed her a plate of Danish she asked, "Can we eat on the balcony?"

153

"Sure. I do that a lot." They took their coffee and Danish to the table and chairs that were tucked into one of the corners overlooking the street.

Candy opened the bakery. She unlocked the door and turned the closed sign over to open. Across the street on Paul's balcony sat Paul and Sam. Candy moved away from the door where she could stare without being seen. She was in shock. He just met the woman, and she spent the night? How could he do that?

Anger did not describe the emotion she was feeling. It was more like a tidal wave of fury coursing through her veins and arteries. Tears pricked at her eyes and spilled down her cheeks. Just two days ago he had been kissing her, and now another woman had spent the night with him. How could he be so heartless? Was he that fickle? If so, she wanted no part of him.

Candy realized she couldn't lie to herself. She missed Paul. She missed Paul a lot. Her own quick temper had ruined their relationship, and now he had moved on. Candy straightened her back, blew her nose, and said to herself, "Be realistic. It's what you do."

Sam worked from Paul's den until Megan called her and told her she was at home with Chip and Jonathan. Sam called to Paul. He came down the hall.

"Everything OK?" he asked.

"Yes. I just got a call from Megan. They're home. I'm going to get some food from the café and take them lunch. Want to come?"

"Sure. I'll help get the food," he said.

Sam packed her car, then she and Paul walked into the café and ordered family packs of barbecue and wings plus two gallons of tea. They placed the food in Paul's car then drove to Chip and Megan's.

Chip helped Paul carry the food in while Sam visited with Megan. When the food was in place, Paul looked over to see Sam rocking Jonathan.

Sam smiled, "I know he should go to his bed, but I love rocking him. Megan, he's just perfect."

Megan said, "You rock him as much as you want. I understand. I love doing that too."

When everyone had fixed a plate of food, Sam put Jonathan in his portable crib and made a plate for herself.

The four ate lunch and laughed at the stories Megan and Sam recalled about playing on their grandparents' farm.

When lunch was over and the kitchen clean, Sam said, "Megan, I need to go. It'll take me five hours to get back to Richmond. I've enjoyed this so much. I need to make more time to come back to Whitlow."

Megan hugged her cousin. "Please do. You're always welcome here."

Sam turned to Paul and said, "It's been wonderful getting to know you, Paul. Thank you for the hospitality. I hope I can return the favor sometime."

"My pleasure, Sam," Paul said, "You're welcome any time. Don't forget your reservation at Halloween."

Sam laughed, "I won't. You can count on that." Sam waved and left.

"Halloween?" Chip asked.

Paul smiled, "Sam liked the balcony. When I told her about watching the children trick-or-treating, she asked if she could come back and watch from the balcony. I said yes."

Paul looked at Megan, "Sam's great. You must've really enjoyed growing up together."

Megan looked wistful, "Yes. It was the best. Did you really let her stay at your place?"

"Yes."

Megan said, "Thank you. I worried about her being in a motel room alone by the interstate. I'm glad she had a safe place to be."

Chapter 23

Paul spent the afternoon working from home and pondering what he should do about the partnership he had with Candy. Finally, he called Rich Hayes and made an appointment.

The next morning, Paul met with Rich. When he left, he had a plan in place and the paperwork needed to make it happen. Paul drove down Main Street and parked behind the bakery. He climbed the back stairs to the third floor, walked through the offices and removed everything but the large furniture. All the files and personal belongings were boxed and loaded into the back of his SUV. When he was finished, he took a deep breath and walked through the back door into the bakery.

The cashier said, "Hi Paul. Do you need to see Candy? She's in the back finishing a cake."

"Thanks, Ellen," he said and walked to the kitchen.

Paul knocked on the door. Candy looked up and saw him standing in the doorway. At first her heart did a flip and she wanted to smile. Then she remembered she was mad at him.

"What can I do for you?" she asked.

"We need to talk, Candy. Can you take a break?"

"I'm in the middle of a cake. Can't it wait?" she asked.

Paul looked at the cake which looked finished to him. In fact, he could tell she was starting her cleanup. Paul knew she was stalling.

Paul pushed his anger to the back of his emotions and said, "Candy, I can tell you're finished and have started cleaning up. Can you please take a moment to look at some papers with me?"

Candy gave an exaggerated sigh. "Alright. Have it your way." She cleaned her hands and said, "What is it?"

"Can we go to your office? It's more private and no one will accidently hear our discussion."

Candy shrugged and walked through the office door and sat at her desk. She pointed to the chair across from her and said, "Have a seat. What's this all about?"

Paul sat down and took the papers out of a small brief-case.

"I had Rich draw up a plan of action for our business."

"What plan of action?" she asked. "I don't remember discussing anything like that."

"We didn't," Paul said.

Candy said sharply, "Oh, is this a secret, too? Like your being my landlord?"

Paul very calmly said, "No. This is nothing like that, but this is a result of your overreaction to the situation."

"Overreaction?" Candy tried hard to stay calm. "I think

I had every right to react the way I did."

Paul took a deep breath. "Candy, I don't want to argue that point any longer. It will not change the fact that I own the company to which you pay rent. Let's get to this paperwork. I have worked out a plan, which Rich will oversee, that outlines a way for you to buy me out of our company."

"Buy you out? What brought this on?"

"Candy, you have not said one civil word to me in the two days since Brian told you I own Blue Ridge Properties. Instead of looking at all the good that has happened since I bought both these buildings, including fixing your café and helping you start your dream bakery, you persist in dwelling on one small fact that has nothing to do with our working together here."

Candy interrupted, "One small fact? Try one big lie."

Paul flushed with anger.

In a calm voice he said, "I never lied to you. Blue Ridge Properties owns that building. We both pay rent to the same company. Now, can we move on to this plan?"

Paul continued, "I will be a very silent partner. I will still fund the company until it makes a significant profit. I want financial statements every two weeks and a quarterly payment from the profits. When you have paid me back for everything I invested, plus ten percent, I will sign my share of the company over to you."

Candy looked at the papers and then at Paul.

"So, this is it? I catch you in a devious behavior, and you

decide to cut and run. I didn't think you were a quitter."

Paul stared at Candy in disbelief. "Candy, do you even hear the venom that comes out of your mouth? I am not quitting. I'm giving you a chance to own the business in full."

"Feels like quitting to me," she said sharply.

Paul stood, "Are you going to sign the papers or not? I'm giving you a very generous offer. You are basically getting my share at cost plus ten percent which is a lot cheaper than most people pay to buy out their partners. I thought you would like to own the bakery yourself just like you own the café."

Candy said nothing in return.

Paul said, "Look these over. Sign them, and I will come get them, or you can give them to Rich yourself. Either way is fine with me."

He paused, then said, "I've cleaned out my offices upstairs. I still own this building, so you'll have to pay rent for the bakery now. The rental fee is stated in the papers. Just give the check to Chip. He'll know where to send it. Also, I plan to rent out the top two floors as soon as I can find a tenant."

"Where are you going?" Candy asked.

"For the time being, I'll revert back to what I was doing, working from home or from wherever I happen to be."

After another pause, Paul said, "I thought we could have a good company and a lot of fun running it together. I even thought I might be starting to have feelings for you.

I have never been more wrong about anything or anyone in my entire life. Let me know your decision." Paul turned and walked out of the office and out the back door.

Candy watched Paul leave. He said he thought he was starting to have feelings for her. Why would he say that now, especially after another woman stayed the night with him? She thought he was a jerk, but that did not stop the tears that finally ran down her cheeks.

Candy sat with her head in her hands. Tears were making her fingers wet. How could this have gone so wrong and so quickly? She knew most of it was her fault, but she couldn't help the hurt she felt when she found out that Paul had kept a secret from her. She also knew it would not have hurt so much if she had not been in love with him.

"Oh, God, help me," she whispered, "I'm in love with Paul Garner, and he can't stand me."

Paul parked behind the café. He took the boxes out of the SUV, carried them up the stairs, and placed them in the spare bedroom. He would sort the items out later. What was he going to do with an extra laptop and printer? Then he thought he should keep them in case he hired another assistant.

Still pondering what to do with the office supplies, Paul took a beer from the refrigerator and went out to the balcony. This was a mistake, he thought. The bakery was right in front of him. Now he couldn't even enjoy his own balcony. He went back inside, took his laptop to his desk and lost himself in the logistic puzzles of his job.

The next afternoon, Paul was sitting in Chip's den holding Jonathan and talking with him and Megan. He told them about his conversation with Candy and his plan to let her buy him out.

Megan said, "I can't believe she could be so self absorbed that she lost sight of the amazing things you've done for her. It seems all she can dwell on are the things she perceived as being deceitful, which they weren't."

"What're you going to do now?" Chip asked.

"Just like before, work from home, and run the logistics company."

He smiled, "Ted is looking for historical properties in this area and Winston. If he finds any good deals, I'll have you look at them to see if they're worth renovating."

"Are you staying in Whitlow?" Megan asked.

"For a few more days. I like hanging out with the little guy here. But I'm going back to Philadelphia for a while. I can't even sit on my balcony without a direct line of vision into the bakery. It's not like we were a romantic item and broke up, but I have never had to defend myself so strongly to someone who didn't want to believe me. That's what stings and makes me angry.

"When time has passed, I'll be back. I'll definitely be back by October before the holidays. Little guy, here, needs to watch a Christmas parade from up high."

Paul stood and handed Jonathan to Megan.

He said, "I may stop in Richmond and see Sam on the way back. I really like her. She has an easy, soothing way about her."

"I know," Megan said. "I love her to bits. If you do stop there, tell her I said hello and to come back to Whitlow for a visit."

Paul reached into his back pocket and pulled out an envelope.

He handed it to Chip and said, "This is Jonathan's baby present. Fill out the paperwork and give it to Rich."

Chip opened the papers, read them and said, "Paul, this is amazing. How can we thank you?"

"Just let me in Jonathan's life. He's the start of the next generation of Garners. I'd like to be around to watch him grow up. The paperwork will make you trustee instead of me. Then leave it alone. By the time he's ready to go to college there should be enough to pay for the first year or two, hopefully more."

Paul hugged Megan and Chip then left.

"What's in the envelope?" Megan asked.

"A mutual fund in Jonathan's name." He showed Megan

the amount.

"Oh, my," Megan said. "If that grows like I think it will, it'll put two kids through college. That's so generous."

"That's so Paul," Chip replied. "Candy is an absolute fool."

Chapter 24

Paul spent the next few days working from his apartment and sorting through the office supplies he had taken from across the street. He kept a few things he could use and looked at the pile of items he didn't need. One thing was clear, he still needed help with the logistics company.

With that decision made, Paul went downstairs to see Tracy. He found her behind the counter watching the café and serving people seated in front of her. Paul took the last stool as was his usual custom.

"Hey there, Paul," she said. "Tea or lunch?"

Paul looked at his watch; it was almost noon. He decided on lunch and gave her his order.

When she came back with his drink he asked, "Has your friend with the computer experience found a job yet?"

"No, not yet. It seems everyone wants the younger, cheaper kids right out of college or technical school," she said.

Paul handed her his business card. "I've already made that mistake. Give him my number and have him call me."

Tracy smiled and took the card.

"You won't regret this. He will be worth every penny you pay him, or you get free tea for a year."

Paul laughed. "Considering how tight you are with Candy's café finances he must really be good."

Tracy said, "I think he is." She looked at him and said, "I thought you were going to leave town."

"I am," Paul replied. "But I still need help. If I hire," Paul paused, "what's his name?"

"Grant," Tracy said. "Grant Sparks."

"Well, if I hire Grant and get him trained, he can work from home, and I can leave town. As long as we communicate every day, we should be good," Paul said.

Two days later, Paul hired Grant and started to train him on how the logistics company worked. Within another two days, Grant recommended stronger, faster computers for Paul to use when he was on the road and was already writing a new program which would connect vendors and freight haulers by identifying lowest cost to vendors and highest profit to the trucking companies.

Paul said to Grant, "You have cut my workload in half. I'm going to give you the primary responsibility of pairing vendors and haulers with maximum profits. This way I can market and personally visit the clients."

Grant chose to work from his home instead of using the offices but agreed that he would work from there if they ever hired more people. With everything in place, Paul called Chip to say goodbye and left Whitlow.

Chapter 25

The following Sunday afternoon, Candy called Megan.

"Megan," she said. "I have a gift for the baby. May I bring it over?"

"Sure, Candy. Come on," Megan said.

A few minutes later, Candy was standing at Megan and Chip's front door with a gift bag on her arm and a meal in her hands.

Chip opened the door. "Here, let me take that," he said, "it looks heavy."

Candy smiled, "Thank you. It's heavy, but I wanted to bring you guys a meal. I understand things are hectic and tiring with a new baby."

"They are," Chip said, "but we wouldn't change a thing. The little guy is amazing. We named him Jonathan. Megan is in the den; why don't you go on in."

Candy walked into the den. Megan was holding Jonathan and rocking him.

"Candy!" she said, smiling. "Come in. It's good to see you."

Candy walked over, handed Megan the baby gift and took a seat in the chair beside her. Megan gently handed Jonathan to Candy and opened the gift.

Candy was holding Jonathan, taking in his features when Megan said, "Thank you, Candy. This is precious." The gift was a collection of stuffed farm animals. "I don't think Allie's baby has these, and he has everything imaginable in the farm toy line."

"I'm glad you like them," Candy said. "I always figure people will get their babies food and clothes but save their money in the toy area."

"You're right about that. Diapers and formula are outrageoulsly expensive. Thank goodness he has taken to breastfeeding."

Megan looked at Candy and said, "Are you alright? You seem a bit down."

Candy replied, "I'm fine. It's been a tough week. Paul and I had a tremendous argument. He wants to dissolve our partnership. I don't know why I'm telling you. I imagine he has told you and Chip everything."

Megan spoke softly and carefully. "Yes. He told us everything from his point of view. An argument has two sides, Candy. Chip and I have not forgotten that. Paul is family, but you're a good friend, too."

Candy smiled as she continued to look at Jonathan.

"Thank you for that." Candy noticed Jonathan had fallen asleep. She handed the baby back to Megan to be put in his bassinette.

Megan said, "Talk to me. How are you doing?"

Candy sighed. "I don't know. I'm still upset that Paul never told me he owned the café's building. If he had been upfront, it wouldn't have mattered. But it's like he didn't trust me or something. That really hurt.

"I know I'm not always easy to be around, but I'm not unreasonable either. It was like a slap in the face that he had done all that work on the café, and I had no idea. I was grateful to the landlord for doing it, but I never said so to Paul. I could have at least told him how much I appreciated it, but he never gave me the chance."

Megan listened with interest. This was a completely different point of view than what Paul had told them.

"Did you tell Paul all this?"

Candy said, "I think I tried, but I was so angry and hurt that I'm sure it didn't come across the way I wanted it to. Then when he wanted me to buy his half of the business so that he didn't have to be around me anymore, well, that hurt even more than not telling me about his owning Blue Ridge Properties. I still have the papers he wants me to sign, but I just can't make myself do it."

A tear rolled down Candy's cheek.

"I messed up so bad, Megan. I don't know how to undo it. But at the same time, Paul has never tried to see my point of view, not once. He just thinks I won't see his point of view.

"He thinks I don't understand business, but I do. I know why he pays rent to Blue Ridge Properties just like I do. I pay rent to our business. I get that. He never got the fact that I was hurt because he didn't trust me to understand and appreciate what he's done for me."

Megan reached for a tissue and handed it to Candy. She said nothing but continued to let Candy talk.

"I really miss him, Megan. I loved working with Paul. We were having a good time planning and making the bakery work. We were getting ready to market the catering business. Now, I just don't care about it. It may have been a dream of mine, but it was our project together." Candy shrugged and more tears fell.

Megan asked, "Candy, do you have feelings for Paul?"

Candy cried harder. "Yes," she squeaked out.

When she calmed, Candy said, "Megan, I fell in love with Paul. I fell in love with a man who cannot trust me, a man who refuses to see my point of view, and a man who will run from me at the first sign of an argument. Heaven help me, but I just don't know how to stop the emotions. How do you fall out of love with someone?"

"I feel awful," Candy continued. "Baking used to be my passion. Now I just go through the motions to keep the display cases full and fulfill orders. I used to experiment with flavors and textures and let Paul decide what to market. It's just not fun anymore. None of it is. I'm sure I will get through this and enjoy the cooking again, but for now..." Candy trailed off, fresh tears running down her face.

Megan took Candy's hand. "I'm so sorry, Candy. I had

no idea how you felt. No one did. All everyone saw was your anger at Paul. No one stopped to ask how you felt, and no one stopped to ask you why you were angry. You just kept everything inside while Paul vented to us, and we assumed he was in the right. He's not completely innocent in all of this. I see that now."

Candy said, "I know I have a temper, but, Megan, when have you ever seen me so angry with anyone? I don't get angry with my staff, my friends, or my family. My anger is triggered when I feel hurt. Paul has the ability to trigger every emotion I have, both good and bad. No one else has that much influence."

Megan looked at her friend with sympathy and compassion.

"What're you going to do now?" she asked.

Candy thought for a moment and said, "Business as usual, I guess. One thing I don't plan to do is sign those papers Paul wants. I'm not ready to divorce him from our partnership. I will send him the financials and his share of the profits. I will send him updates on the business, but I will not make it easy for him to leave it."

"I think that's a good plan, Candy. I really do," Megan said. "Maybe with a little time you'll both regain interest and energy for the project you started together."

Candy said, "Speaking of work, when you decide to return, I need an accountant for the bakery."

Megan smiled, "Bring me your reports and statements. I never really stopped working. I just work from here."

Candy said, "Thanks."

She stood and said, "Thank you for listening, but I've taken enough of your time. Stop by the bakery. We'll have a cup of coffee and a cupcake, my treat."

Megan smiled, "I'll do that."

Megan walked Candy to the door, hugged her and said, "Thank you for the toys, and remember, we are still your friends."

Candy hugged Megan tightly. "Thank you," she said and left.

Paul drove out of Whitlow and turned north on the interstate to go to Philadelphia. He was both sad and relieved to be leaving. He didn't really want to leave Chip and his family, but he couldn't stand to see the bakery outside his window all day, every day.

He just didn't get why Candy couldn't understand that his businesses outside the bakery were his private property and that he didn't have to tell anyone anything about them. She took it way too personally, he thought. And her reaction to his proposal for her to buy him out, well, one would've thought they were married and that he'd asked for a divorce. She had overreacted on every aspect of their situation. Paul ignored the fact that while he was glad to be leaving Whitlow because of Candy, he already missed her.

An hour into his drive, Paul decided to detour east to Richmond. A day or two there in the company of Samantha Albright was just what he needed. She was calm, easy to be around, and she had become a good friend.

Paul arrived in Richmond and took Sam to dinner at her favorite restaurant which was on the waterfront of the James River. Afterward, they strolled along the Riverwalk. The evening had been enjoyable with an easy flow of conversation.

Finally, Sam said, "What are you going to do about Whitlow and your relationship with Candy? It seems you left things unresolved there. You won't rest easy until all your loose ends have been woven back into the tapestry of your comfort zone."

Paul chuckled, "You get right to the point, don't you. I think I've resolved it. I've given Candy a way to buy me out of the business. What more could she want?"

Sam asked, "Has she signed the papers? Is it a sure thing?"

"I don't know," Paul said. "I left them with her to sign and give to the lawyer. I haven't heard from Rich, so I don't know the status of the paperwork."

"Do you think it's possible that she might not want to end the business relationship with you?" she asked.

"Why wouldn't she? She can't stand me."

"I don't know, Paul. There's a fine line between the different emotions. When someone sparks the level of anger that you say she had, then that same someone could just as easily trigger stronger positive emotions like love and loyalty. Maybe that's why she was so angry. If she had feelings for you, she would've been hurt that you couldn't share the truth with her and hurt sometimes triggers the harshest of anger."

For a moment Paul was stunned at the possibility of what Sam had said, but he dismissed it.

"No," he said, "I can't see it. If she had feelings for me, she would not have reacted that way in the beginning."

"I wouldn't be too sure about that," Sam replied.

Paul started to get annoyed with Sam's championing of Candy's viewpoint. "What makes you so sure?" he asked.

Sam smiled, "I have a double major, business and psychology. The psychology part gives me an insight into behavior. Fortunately, I can use the information to help the company I work for. Sometimes, though, I don't always like what I can read in people's conversation, behavior, and body language."

The two had circled back along the cobblestone street to the parking deck where their cars were.

Sam said, "Paul, I really like you. You're the type of man I would love to have a long-term relationship with. However, I believe that you have feelings for Candy. I think you're trying to deny those feelings, but I can see that they are still there. I would also bet that Candy has feelings for you."

Sam gave Paul a sad smile. "If you figure all of this out and you decide you really don't have feelings for Candy, I would love to see you again. But I'm smart enough to not want to see a man who has the ghost of feelings left for someone else. I am selfish enough to want to be the absolute only in a man's life."

Sam gave Paul a hug and said, "Goodbye, Paul. Give Chip and Megan my best. I'm sure I'll see you again in Whitlow. Take care."

Paul watched Sam get in her car and drive away. He liked Sam, but he wasn't devastated when she drove out of his life. He was also convinced that she was wrong about his having feelings for Candy. The only thing he felt toward Candy was anger, hurt, and annoyance.

Candy flipped through the channels on the television. In frustration, she just turned it off and started to cry again. She bent over and cried out her feelings.

She prayed, "Oh, God, why do I have to be so quick to anger, quick to hurt? Why do I feel like I have to control cvery situation, and why couldn't Paul trust me with the truth? How do I get through this and run a business? How do I get over being in love with a man who doesn't love me back? God, I need you. I need your peace and forgiveness. Help me to change, Lord. Help me to be a better person."

Candy continued to pour out her heartbreak to God. Eventually, she sat up, dried her eyes and blew her nose. She smiled as she realized she felt more peaceful than she had in days. No, more like months or years. It made her sad to realize that this was probably the first time she had ever let go of a situation and let God direct the course of her life. She already felt God changing her.

She smiled and prayed, "Thank you."

Chapter 26

As the weeks passed, word of Candy's skills in baking spread through the adjacent towns and counties. She took a contract position with Wilkes County Community College to teach a baking class in the food sciences division.

The current summer session was the first class she would be supervising in a skills lab setting at the college. In the fall semester, she would teach the fundamentals of yeast, flour, sugars, and kneading to students in the classroom. They would complete their baking labs with her in Whitlow at the bakery. Candy knew she would have to work earlier in the mornings and later in the evenings on the days she was teaching, but she was excited about the prospect of working with students who were interested in the same things she was.

Candy was nervous when she walked into the kitchen lab at the college. However, once she started demonstrating and watching the students learn skills, her nervousness left, and she enjoyed the experience. The two-hour lab period passed quickly. While the students were glad to be finished, she was almost sad, but it told her she would enjoy the process of teaching others.

By October, Candy had settled into a routine that was comfortable and rewarding. One of the college students who showed an interest in baking agreed to work for her in the bakery three evenings a week. It was good to have extra help keeping the display cases full while continuing to complete custom orders.

People started taking day trips from the surrounding larger cities to see Whitlow, eat at the café, and enjoy sweet treats from the bakery. Candy delayed starting the catering company because the bakery was so busy. The good part was that she only thought of Paul once or twice a day instead of all day, every day.

Candy also noticed a change in her behavior toward others. She was more patient, slower to anger, happier, and never thought about manipulating anyone. She thanked God daily for the changes he was making in her. What Candy didn't realize was that everyone else had noticed the changes in her, too.

The days were getting shorter, and the evenings were getting cooler. Candy turned the bakery sign to closed and turned out the lights. The streetlights were already on, but Candy still noticed a light on in Paul's apartment. She sighed. He said he would be back for the holidays. Just when she began to believe life without Paul was bearable, he came back to town. Well, maybe she wouldn't run into him, but she knew that was wishful thinking. Whitlow was too small, and she still had not signed the papers that would allow him to leave the business through a buyout.

Paul finished the last bite of pecan pie and said, "That was delicious, Megan. Thanks for the meal."

He smiled at Jonathan who was sitting in a highchair trying to put pieces of cereal in his mouth.

"I can't believe how much he has grown," Paul said.

"We can't either," Chip replied. "I swear that if I blink, he grows another half inch."

Paul chuckled, "I can believe it."

"Are you glad to be back in Whitlow?" Chip asked.

"It's OK. I like the apartment, and it is handy to be close to Grant. That guy is amazing. He completely re-structured the schedules, lowered the vendor's costs, and increased the freight hauler's profit. As a result, I'm getting more calls from companies wanting our services. Grant is handling the volume of work like a champ which gives me the chance to visit customers and even do some marketing."

After a lull in the conversation, Megan asked, "Have you seen Candy?"

Paul grimaced and sighed, "No. I've been putting that off. She still hasn't signed the papers agreeing to buy my part of the business. She sends statements every month and profits every quarter. Evidently, she's doing well."

"That would be an understatement," Megan said. "She has people coming from all the cities around just to eat at the café and visit the bakery. The college in Wilkes County has contracted with her to teach baking in their food science program. She's even hired a part-time person to help her three afternoons a week. I don't know how she keeps up with everything."

"I still don't want to have to deal with her," Paul said.

Megan asked, "Paul, have you even tried to understand why she reacted the way she did? Or have you decided that she's totally wrong and that you're totally right?"

Paul frowned, "What are you saying, Megan, that I've been unfair? Tell that to the woman who spews venom whenever I'm around."

"Yes, Paul. That is what I am saying. You are so wrapped up in your own feelings of pride that you have failed to see why Candy reacted the way she did."

Paul responded sarcastically, beginning to get angry, "And I suppose you know why she is so short tempered, hateful and untrusting?"

"Yes, I do know," Megan answered.

When Megan did not elaborate, Paul said, "Well? What's the problem besides the fact that she has a personality disorder?"

"Paul, listen to yourself. You are spewing the very venom you claim Candy does. You're not willing to give her the benefit of the doubt on any level. I do know why she reacted so strongly, but I also know you need to ask her yourself. You two need to talk this out."

Before Paul could respond she said, "Now, I am going to take Jonathan into his bedroom and put him to bed. You hang out with your brother without my interference. Before you get too angry with me Paul, remember, you are family and I love you. I only want what is best for you which is to resolve this and put it behind you." Megan kissed him on the cheek. "Goodnight."

Paul watched her leave the room. He looked at Chip who heard the whole conversation.

Paul asked, "I suppose you think she's right?"

Chip looked back at Paul and said, "Maybe. I don't have any answers for you, Bro. You're on your own, here. I can't help you with Candy because it's your set of problems, and I won't interfere or give advice."

Paul rolled his eyes and said, "Some helpful brother you are."

Chip grinned, "I think I'm more helpful than you know. Now, tell me about this Halloween thing you want to do."

Chapter 27

Paul was standing in front of the door to his balcony drinking coffee and just staring at the street. Candy came out of the bakery and stood on the sidewalk looking at the windows. Ellen came out and they talked, pointed at something in the windows, and measured the outside. What was she doing? She better not do any construction without his permission.

A few minutes later he was relieved when he saw they were hanging Halloween decorations. She had on blue jeans that hugged her curves. Her t-shirt had the picture of a cotton boll with the name Cotton Bakery on it. Ellen wore an identical one, but it didn't have the same effect as Candy's had. Candy looked like she had been poured into the shirt. Paul was angry with himself. He didn't want to find her attractive and desirable, and he sure as heck didn't want to admit he missed her.

Paul watched a young man come up to them and speak to Candy. She smiled and motioned him into the bakery. Must be a customer. Fifteen minutes later, the man had not come out of the building. What was going on?

Two young college age women entered the building. After several minutes they were still inside. He hoped they were buying a lot of coffee and doughnuts for the large amount of time they were using table space. Ellen came back out and placed a small haybale and pumpkins in the outside corner of the entrance.

Disgusted with himself, Paul went to his bedroom to get some work done. Unable to concentrate, he took his laptop into the dining area where he could see the bakery. Over the course of the morning, a steady stream of customers came and went.

A church van parked on Main Street. A group got out and went into the café. An hour later, the same group walked across the street to the bakery. When they came out, every person had either a box or a bag of purchases from inside. Now he understood the financial statements he had received. Candy had managed to make the café and the bakery a successful packaged deal.

Candy knew Paul was back in town because she had seen the lights on in his apartment every night. She suspected he was watching the bakery during the day. Candy grinned to herself; if he had decided to spy on her business, she would give him something to see. She wore the tightest jeans and t-shirt she owned to work.

Candy wore a smock and hair net when she worked in the kitchen, and she required the students to do the same when they came in for their skills lab. They were currently across the street at the café for lunch while their recipes were rising in the warmer.

Candy ate a quick salad, took off the smock and hairnet, picked up her broom and went out to the sidewalk. She and Ellen always made sure their section of the street was neat and tidy, but today she made a show of it. She could feel Paul watching. He had found her attractive before their argument, maybe he would again, and maybe he would come over.

The students finished their lab, and Paul watched as they left with a bag each. Megan had told him about Candy's contract with the community college, which was obviously working out well. On top of that, Tracy informed him that she took group reservations at the café for the back dining room two or three times a week.

At the rate Candy was going, she would be able to buy him out sooner than he had thought. But why did that bother him, and why was he a little relieved she hadn't signed those papers? Had he been too hasty in his anger? And why could he not take his eyes off her when she was sweeping the sidewalk?

Paul looked at his watch. The bakery closed in thirty minutes. It was dark outside, but anyone could see inside because of the light shining through the windows casting odd shades of yellow onto the sidewalk. Ellen had left. Candy was emptying the display cases and securing the food for the night. Paul watched as Officer Hank walked into the bakery and started talking with Candy. She bagged a few items and handed them to the policeman. He handed her money, and she gave him change. They talked a little longer, and Candy put a Halloween cookie in a bag and gave it to him. What was that about?

Swearing to himself, Paul could stand it no longer. He walked downstairs, through the café, and across the street. He spoke to Officer Hank who was leaving. Paul turned the sign around to closed and locked the door.

"I'm supposed to be open for another five minutes," Candy said calmly. "My partner might be upset if I miss a customer." This time there was a hint of humor in her voice. He was surprised.

"Your partner will understand," he said.

Paul walked over to the counter. "How are you, Candy?"

Candy smiled, "I'm good. As a matter of fact, I am very good. How are you?"

Paul answered, "I'm good, too. Your business seems to be booming."

"Yes," Candy said. "I'm pleased with how it's going. We have established a routine. New customers and a few regulars come in the afternoon for fresh items. A few regulars come in the morning for the day old mark downs. It works," she said.

"Obviously. Your profit statements are impressive for a business less than a year old," Paul said.

A voice from the kitchen interrupted them. "Candy, I'm here."

Candy smiled, "Come meet Haley."

Candy led Paul to the kitchen where he saw a teenage girl fixing her hair into a bun and putting on a hairnet. She already had on a work smock.

Candy said, "Paul, this is Haley. She helps me three evenings during the week, and sometimes she comes in on a Saturday. She makes the cinnamon rolls and the muffin batter. I get them out of the refrigerator early in the morning and bake them. Hot muffins and cinnamon rolls are ready when the doors open.

"We get a lot of breakfast-on-the-go business. I take some of the cinnamon rolls and muffins over to the café. The owner of the coffee shop at the interstate buys two dozen of each every morning."

Candy turned to Haley and said, "Haley, this is Paul Garner. He's my business partner. You haven't met him because he's been out of town. The bakery is only one of several businesses he owns and juggles. Successfully, I might add."

"Hi, Mr. Garner," Haley said. "It's nice to meet you."

"It's nice to meet you, too, Haley. How did you happen to come to work here?" he asked.

"Candy taught a baking lab at the school last summer. I graduate in May from the food science program. She saw I liked to bake, and we seemed to get along, so here I am."

Candy smiled, "I really don't know what I would do without her. Go ahead and start the yeast dough, Haley. I need to talk with Paul. I'll be right back."

Candy turned to Paul, "Want to talk? We can go in my office. Or if you don't want to talk, I'll let you out the front door."

"I want to talk, Candy, but now is not a good time for you. When do you have spare time?" he asked.

"Sundays. And I don't mean to sound flippant. It's my only day off. However, there's a slump between ten and one every day. You can come over then if you like. Ellen can take care of things while we talk."

Paul said, "Alright. I'll see you tomorrow sometime between ten and one."

He turned to go out the door but stopped and asked, "What do you do while Haley works?"

Candy grinned, "I have a birthday cake to decorate which will be picked up tomorrow. Then I have a batch of pumpkin cookies to decorate. I finished the ghost cookies this afternoon. Tomorrow I'll get the witches done. They're for a Halloween party someone is having Friday night."

Paul looked at Candy closely and asked, "When do you sleep?"

Candy said, "At night of course."

Paul chuckled, "Why did I ask? I'll see you tomorrow. Lock the door behind me."

Paul walked back across the street and into the café. Tracy was washing the counter and getting ready to close for the night.

"Took you long enough," she said as he walked by.

"Don't you start, too," he said gruffly as he walked away. He heard Tracy laughing as he went up the stairs.

Paul walked into the apartment, got a beer, and plopped on the couch. Why had he ever thought he could forget Candy Cotton? She was more attractive now than the first day he met her, and she still had that wit that could make him laugh, even when he was mad. He was glad Haley had come into the kitchen. He wasn't sure how long he could have held out before he took Candy into his arms and kissed her. What in heaven's name was he going to do?

Chapter 28

P aul watched the clock and watched the customers going in and out of the bakery. Candy was telling the truth about the breakfast to-go crowd. He bet every one of those people carried either a muffin or a cinnamon roll in their bag along with a cup of coffee. He had noticed the coffee urns with varying labels sitting next to the display case. He would have to ask her about that.

Finally, it was ten. Paul closed his laptop, went down the stairs, through the café, across the street, and into the bakery.

Candy smiled when she saw him come into the store. "Ellen, could you take care of things while Paul and I talk?"

"Sure. Don't worry." Ellen replied.

Candy gave Ellen a large smile and said, "I never do."

She turned to Paul and said, "Let's go to my office."

Paul followed her into the room and shut the door. He watched Candy calmly walk around the desk to her chair before taking his own seat.

"What do you want to know?" she asked.

"Why haven't you signed the papers?" he asked.

Candy took a deep breath. "Because I can't afford to buy you out. If that day comes, and you still want out, we can negotiate everything then. Right now, it seems pointless."

Candy paused then took a chance.

She said, "And I was hoping we could get back on the right foot with each other and continue as amicable partners."

"You did?" he asked.

"I was hoping, yes," she answered.

"Why?"

Candy searched for the right words.

"In the beginning, we had a good time putting the bakery together. We think alike when it comes to business. I thought we made a good team and was hoping we could continue that."

Paul listened. "So, you got over being angry?"

"Yes," she said. "I suppose I owe you an apology for some of the things I said. I really can't remember all the conversations. I understand that Blue Ridge Properties is the owner of the building. The problem was my assumption that we were close enough that you could've told me you own Blue Ridge Properties. I would've understood."

Candy paused then said, "I was hurt that you didn't think you could trust me with that information. You trusted Chip and Megan with it, why not me. That was my thought process. Anyway, I never get that angry unless I feel hurt. So, I'm sorry. I thought enough of you that I was hurt. It's that simple. I understand if you can't get past this and the things I said, but I hope that someday you can understand and forgive my thin skin."

Paul said, "Thank you for explaining. Megan told me I needed to ask you for myself. She said she knew why you were angry but was holding it in confidence."

Candy smiled, "Megan's a good friend. She let me vent, talk, and even cry."

"Cry?" he asked incredulously. "You cried?"

"Yes. You were my friend and business partner. I let my feelings get the better of me and drove you away. I was sad."

"You were sad?" he asked.

"Very."

"Candy, I...." Paul stopped. He wanted to hug her and kiss her, but he knew he dare not do that until he could understand his own feelings.

"I'm not sure what to say. I never pictured you being sad over this."

"I was."

Paul stood. "Tear the papers up. You were right. It was premature and pointless to try to make you decide to buy me out. I did that because I was angry with you."

He turned to leave. "I need to let you get back to work, but I'll be back. We need to talk about why you haven't started the catering business." Paul left her office and the bakery.

Candy let her breath out. She felt like a weight that had been sitting on her chest for almost six months had lifted. She smiled as she tore the papers in two.

Paul could not concentrate on his job. All he could think about was Candy's apology and that she confessed to being sad that he had left town. She admitted her weakness and admitted to why she lost her temper. She admitted everything and even asked for his forgiveness. She had bared her soul and asked that they remain partners. Candy had nothing left to hide. She had laid everything out on the table, including missing their friendship.

What had he admitted? What had he shared with her? Nothing. Absolutely nothing. He had taken her good will, given her nothing in return, and she took it with grace.

Paul suddenly felt ashamed. He thought he had been the better person, and Candy had been in the wrong. But Candy was right. He had expected her to give her all, even share information about the café to make the business work. Megan had been right to champion Candy. Paul put his head in his hands, took a deep breath, and tried to figure out how to fix this mess.

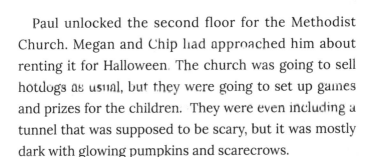

Paul unlocked the second floor for the Methodist Church. Megan and Chip had approached him about renting it for Halloween. The church was going to sell hotdogs as usual, but they were going to set up games and prizes for the children. They were even including a tunnel that was supposed to be scary, but it was mostly dark with glowing pumpkins and scarecrows.

Paul went down the stairs to the bakery. He handed Candy a key to the second floor.

"Would you mind keeping this? That way they don't have to chase me down to unlock the door whenever they want to get in. You're here all the time, so it should be convenient."

Candy smiled, "Of course I'll let them in. I love their plan. I'm donating Halloween cookies to go with the hotdogs and bringing an urn of coffee for the adults who don't want soft drinks. I'm also making small cookies to give out to the children for Halloween instead of candy. Maybe their parents will buy something while they're here."

Paul said, "Smart ideas, Candy." Paul stopped talking

when Hank Bowen walked in.

He asked, "Does Officer Hank come every day?"

"Almost," Candy said. "I'll be right back."

Candy went to the display case and asked, "Do you want the usual or something else?"

"The usual will be fine. Thank you, Candy," Hank answered.

Paul watched Candy fill a bag with several muffins. She picked out three Halloween cookies and put them in another bag.

"Here you go, Hank. Don't let the kids know about the cookies. Put it in their lunches tomorrow as a surprise."

"Thank you, Candy. They'll be excited and the envy of their classmates." Hank paid her.

Then she said, "Wait here."

Candy went to the kitchen and came back with two take-out boxes and handed them to Hank.

"We had these left over. If they're not eaten today, I'll have to throw them out. Take them home for dinner. That way Donna can rest without worrying about preparing a meal."

Hank seemed speechless, "I can pay you, Candy."

"No. You take them. I gave some others away, but I saved these for you. I hope you enjoy them."

Hank took the boxes and said, "Thank you. I know Donna will be grateful for this. She stays so tired." Almost unable to speak, Hank picked up the bags and carried everything out of the store.

When Hank was gone, Paul came up and said, "What's going on? You gave him fresh muffins at the day old price, free cookies and those were fresh meals from the to-go business, not leftovers. Not that I mind, it's your business. I'm just curious."

Candy got a sad look on her face. "Hank's wife is having chemotherapy for cancer. She can't work. She can't do the things around the house she normally does, and it all falls on Hank.

"He gets the muffins because the kids like them. Donna does too. I give them cookies as a treat. They're having a hard time on just one income, so that's why I give him a break. He asks for six muffins, but I give him seven. I actually come out better because he makes sure the bakery and café are safe at night. He's a good man."

Paul nodded in understanding. Why had he ever thought Candy was self-centered and selfish? She was showing herself to be generous and giving. He was beginning to believe he had never known the real Candy. She had more layers and goodness than he ever thought.

Chapter 29

I t was Halloween. Paul sat on the balcony watching the children running up and down the street. Candy was dressed like a cartoon baker with a puffy middle and a fake mustache. He noticed that a lot of parents bought cookies as they left the building after getting hot dogs on the second floor. Several children came out of the building with small stuffed animals that they had apparently won in a game.

Paul planned to give Chip a break on the room fee. He would charge just enough to cover the expenses for electricity and clean-up. Hopefully the open space would catch on for more rentals. He needed Candy to start the catering business. The second floor would be a perfect venue.

Paul sat in the dark as the crowds thinned in downtown Whitlow. Through the windows he could see the volunteers cleaning up the food and games on the second floor. He could see Candy taking the money out of the register and bagging the leftover Halloween sweets for quick sale the next day. She had removed her costume and worked in a pair of shorts and a t-shirt. He had never noticed what great legs the woman had.

Paul couln't take it anymore. He got up, ran down the stairs and through the café.

As he was going out the door Tracy yelled, "That door will be locked in ten minutes."

Paul called back, "No worries."

Paul walked across the street. Candy had locked the bakery door, but he had a key. He let himself in. She saw him so he knew he would not startle her.

"What's wrong, Paul?" she asked. "You look like a man on a mission."

"Are you through for the night?" he asked.

"Yes. I was just getting ready to leave. Why?"

Paul turned out the dining area lights, went with her to the kitchen and turned out those lights. The only illumination was from the security lights and her office. Paul took her hand, drew her to him and kissed her. He kissed her with an urgency, like a thirsty man in the desert drinks water.

At first Candy was startled, then joy filled her heart, and she kissed him back. She kissed him with all the longing she had felt for the last six months. She kissed him with all the love she had in her heart.

Paul broke the kiss but held her to him and whispered in her ear. "I'm sorry, too, Candy. I should've trusted you with the same level of disclosure that you trusted me with the café. If I had not been so self-righteously sure

I was right and you were wrong, I could have saved both of us six months of misery. I've missed you, Candy. I've missed you so much."

Candy felt her heart soar. "I have thought of you every single day since you left town. At first it was with hurt and anger, then sorrow. After a while I thought of you fondly only once or twice a day, not the day long misery that it was in the beginning. But I never stopped missing you."

Paul said, "There's no way we can completely start over, but do you think we could start again from today?"

"I would like that, Paul," she said.

Paul sighed with relief and kissed her again.

Chapter 30

C andy felt exhausted. Paul had taken her to lunch after church, and now she was staring at the gas logs in his apartment. She had so many orders for cakes and cookies for Christmas parties that she could barely keep up. Ellen had done the Christmas decorating in the bakery by herself. Haley had finished her exams and was now working every day, but it was still hard to keep up.

Paul looked at her. "When are you going to hire extra help?

"I did. Haley. She's full time part time if that makes sense. The pressure will drop off the week of Christmas when all the parties are over. I have a few orders for cakes to be picked up before noon on Christmas Eve. Then business will come to a standstill. It'll be light until Valentines."

Candy yawned, "Haley will start full time with benefits when she finishes her last exam in May. We're both excited about it. She's a good kid and has a lot of potential. I'm going to turn the muffins over to her first, then cupcakes. I want to work on pastries. It's been a while since I tried those."

Paul smiled, "Always the lady with a plan."

Candy smiled with her eyes closed, "Yep."

Candy did not even realize she had fallen asleep. Paul put a pillow under her head and a light blanket over her. He sat in his recliner lightly dozing.

When Candy woke, it was dark. The only light in the apartment came from the gas logs, and the television that was quietly playing a football game.

She sat up momentarily confused then asked, "How long did I sleep?"

"A couple hours."

"I'm sorry. I must be a real bore," she said.

"Not at all," Paul said. "I took a short nap then turned on the game. Philadelphia is playing."

Paul moved over to the couch and pulled Candy into his arms.

"You needed the rest. I'm glad you felt comfortable enough here to get it."

"But I missed time with you," she whined.

Paul chuckled, "I would rather have you rested than tired. Are you hungry? I have two meals Tracy gave me last night in the refrigerator."

Candy laughed. "Is Tracy feeding you now?"

"Only the food she would have to throw out because they're closed on Sunday," he answered.

"That makes sense," she said. "Let's see what she gave you."

Candy reheated the food, and they ate at the kitchen island. She laughed at the blinking Christmas tree.

"Still have your designer decorations, I see."

"Yep. My nod to the holidays. It goes back in the box the day after Christmas," Paul replied, grinning.

"At least no one can call you Scrooge," she said. "I mean, you do have one decoration."

"Maybe next year I'll decorate more. I've been thinking about buying a house," he said.

Candy looked shocked. "You with a house? I thought you hated yardwork."

"I do, but I can hire someone for that. I'm beginning to get a little claustrophobic here. Plus, I would like to have a bigger outdoor living space."

"That sounds nice," Candy said. "Where are you looking?"

Paul said, "There's a farm for sale out near Allie and Jacob. Chip and I are going to buy it and split it. Megan wants the old farmhouse for Chip to restore. I'll build a new, modern, totally out of place house. Or maybe a house that resembles an old farmhouse. I haven't decided yet."

"That sounds wonderful, Paul. You and Chip will be near each other. Chip and Jacob will be near each other, and Megan and Allie will be near each other with children the same age. It's like something out of a story book. What will you do with the farmland?"

"Rent it to Allie," he said. "There's a great pond on the

property. Chip and I used to love to go fishing with our dad. Chip can teach Jonathan and make the circle of life complete."

Candy sighed, "I think I'm a little jealous of y'all living near each other. I can just picture the trails made by all the ATVs you guys will have."

"So, you would like to live out there?" he asked.

"Duh, does a cat climb trees? It sounds idyllic," she said.

"What kind of house would you build if it were yours?" he asked.

"I would build a nice modern home that looked like an old farmhouse with a porch that wraps around three sides. The fourth side is the garage of course. Lots of living spaces, lots of bedrooms and bathrooms."

"Sounds big," Paul said.

"Yes. It would have to be to house all the children," Candy replied, smiling.

"Children?" he asked.

"Yes. Lots," Candy said, grinning bigger.

"How many is lots?" he asked.

"Oh, I would settle for three or four."

"So, you would be happy if I built a large farmhouse that would house lots of children?" Paul asked.

"It's your house, Paul. You build what you want," Candy told him.

"What if I want what you want?"

"Then I would be a great help while you plan."

"What if I want you to live there with me?" he asked.

Candy stilled. "Are you asking me to move in with you?"

Paul looked at Candy, took her hand and said, "Yes. But first, will you marry me?"

Candy felt her eyes well with tears and her heart soar with happiness. She said, "Yes."

Paul said softly, "You know I love you, right?"

"Yes. But I would like to hear it."

Paul stood, took Candy in his arms and said, "Candy Cotton, I love you. Will you marry me?"

Candy saw the love reflected in Paul's eyes. She smiled, knowing he could see the love in hers. She said, "Paul Garner, I love you, too, and yes. I will marry you."

They sealed the deal with a kiss. Then more kisses.

Paul and Candy got married in the chapel of the Methodist Church the Saturday after Valentine's Day. It was a small wedding with only family and close friends present. Chip and Megan provided a light supper after the ceremony.

After Paul and Candy left for their honeymoon, Allie turned to Megan and said, "Well, she did it."

"Did what?" asked Megan.

"Changed her name. She's no longer Cotton, Candy on any roll books."

Epilogue

G rant Sparks opened his refrigerator and got a beer. He had just gotten home from the wedding. The only person he knew there was Tracy, but he still appreciated Paul inviting him.

He had only worked for Paul about eight months. In that small amount of time, Grant had come to respect Paul's creativity, vision, and business acumen. Working for Garner Logistics was the best job he ever had.

Grant took a drink of his beer and sighed. Paul and Candy had looked so happy. Here he was, in his mid thirties, sitting on his couch alone. Grant wondered if he would ever be as fortunate to find the perfect wife. He could always hope.

Coming in 2024: *An Unforseen Danger.* The story of life in Whitlow continues in book 3 of the series.

Also By A. K. Gentry

.

An Awkward Inheritance, Book 1 of the Whitlow Series

Blog: brushymountainwisdom.blogspot.com, a series of short stories set near the fictional town of Whitlow.

Coming soon: *The Perfect Loophole*, a story about the age old battle between good and evil.

About the Author

A. K. Gentry grew up in rural North Carolina. She has lived in or outside small towns most of her adult life. *An Unlikely Partnership* draws on her love of small towns where there is usually a café where friends run into each other. The book also expresses her love of family and faith. Gentry is a retired registered nurse. She is married, has two daughters, one son in law, two granddaughters, and two granddogs.

Printed in the USA
CPSIA information can be obtained
at www.ICGtesting.com
LVHW041240111023
760672LV00048B/759